DEADLY DECEIT

DEADLY DECEIT

JAY DIX

ais
Academic Information Systems, Inc

©Academic Information Systems, 2001

All rights reserved. No part of this publication may be reproduced, stored in a retrieval system, or transmitted in any form without written permission of the publisher. For information address: Academic Information Systems, Inc. 5609 St. Charles Rd. Columbia, MO 65202 USA. Phone: 1-573-474-8161, Fax: 1-573-474-6737, email: aiscolmo@aol.com

For ordering and customer service, call 1-573-474-8161

Printed in the United States of America

— To Mary —

1

The blast from my gun was deafening. I thought I had fired the first shot, but my body was hurled backwards as the noise of the explosion was still registering. I heard my back snap as I hit the rear door handle of my car. Slumping to the ground, I ended up in a semi-reclining position against the cool metal. Even though I was dazed, I saw that my shot had found its mark.

My victim lay motionless on the ground. The tips of his shoes, pointed skyward, looked abnormally large from my viewpoint. I turned my attention to the downed man's associate. This was my true enemy, the man who was responsible for wrecking my life. I had succeeded in stopping his bodyguard, but unfortunately, my enemy was still alive.

He had hesitated during the shooting, but now he bent down and retrieved his fallen comrade's gun. I could see the sickening smile on his face after he rose and headed towards me.

"This is going to be easier than I'd anticipated," he snarled, raising the gun and pointing it at me. The muzzle, from my vantage point, looked like a cannon. "You're going to die a miserable, slow, suffering death for all the trouble you've caused me. You're not going to pin his death on me."

I glanced down at my right side. Miraculously, my gun was still in my hand. But I couldn't lift my arm. Looking over at my right shoulder, I realized blood was seeping through the material in my sleeve. I must have been shot. For some reason, I began to think about the tragic possibility of a permanently disabled arm and not about the man who was walking towards me. I attempted another arm movement, but heard only the grating of splintered bones as I tried to shift my shoulder.

As I reached over my body with my left arm to grab the useless gun, my assailant deftly kicked it out of my hand and sent it careening across the pavement. All I could do was helplessly follow its progress sliding down the road where it came to rest many feet away. Now I was completely helpless. Death suddenly seemed very close at hand, and the hatred I felt for this malicious thug began to bubble up in my veins.

He bent down within a foot of my face and sneered menacingly, "I'm going to thoroughly enjoy this!"

I watched his trigger finger tighten almost imperceptibly. The air became a soundless vacuum, and I pondered quite objectively the fact that my life was now ending. Fear evaporated. I was overcome with a strange sense of relief. I closed my eyes and waited for the inevitable. The roar of the erupting gun was no surprise.

Suddenly a huge weight landed on my legs, followed by a wheezing exhalation of breath. I couldn't move my legs.

"Doc? Doc? It's over now. Are you all right?" The voice of Gus Crider, the homicide detective I'd worked with for over five years, pierced my fuzzy consciousness. I struggled to open my eyes but the lids were gooey and heavy. Then the crunching weight on my legs surprisingly lifted, and I could see the vague outline of Gus dragging a body across the pavement. He was groaning with the effort and finally just shoved the body into a heap next to the other one.

I focused on Gus's considerable paunch which had grown over the years from a little softness to a large tire. He'd been eating too many doughnuts and way too much pasta. His excess flesh loomed directly overhead as he peered into my face. An eternally soggy and always unlit cigar hung from his lips. Good old Gus, he'd stuck with his non-smoking plan for at least six months now.

He yanked his handkerchief from his pocket and then put a very unpleasant pressure on my shoulder as he spoke softly, "Doc, I've got to get you some help. I'll be back as soon as I can."

I tried to answer, but the words wouldn't form. My tongue was huge in my mouth. His footsteps retreated into the quiet. Later, I heard other steps, but they were all unfamiliar. I was frustrated that my mind wasn't working the way it should. Dizziness kept attacking my efforts at lucidity. The last thing I remembered was seeing the bodies on the pavement in front of me and wondering how I'd ever manage to get two autopsies done if my arm was paralyzed.

I AWOKE TO THE UNFAMILIAR SMELL of disinfectant. It was a far cry from the formalin that permeated the atmosphere in my office. My head was muddled, but I knew I was in a hospital room. The glaring whiteness and the smiling countenance of my assistant, Karen, shocked me into consciousness. My thoughts drifted back to the first day Karen had come to work with me. Young and eager, she had all the enthusiasm of a beginning doctor ready to change the world. Now a year later, she was still enthusiastic, but the gritty realities of forensic pathology had tempered her naive idealism. Bartholomew Williamson, one of the best medical examiners in the country, had trained her. Now past his prime for performing autopsies, he was still a fine teacher and as Karen's mentor, his meticulous training was clearly evident.

The deep red suit Karen was wearing offset the room's harsh sterility. Next to Karen, his brow knitted with concern, stood the ever trusty Gus.

"Well . . . it's about time you came around," stated Karen solicitously. "How do you feel?"

"It's a little hard to tell since I just woke up."

"At least his humor is intact," Gus responded.

"How long have I been here?"

Karen volunteered the medical particulars. "Yesterday, you were taken to surgery from the E.R. The operation took a few hours, but everything went well. You lost a considerable amount of blood, both at the scene of the shooting and then here in the hospital. The bullet nicked the subclavian artery and shattered your clavicle. Those were pretty easy to repair. Your tenth vertebrae was fractured and it had to be fused to eleven. There was no apparent damage to your spinal cord according to Dr. Klein, your neurosurgeon. You were given the usual dose of painkillers. You've been unconscious for almost 24 hours."

I tried to shift on the pillow, but my shoulder ached and my legs were numb. My grimace was obvious to both Gus and Karen.

"Don't try to move your legs. They won't be working correctly yet," Karen admonished in her clinical doctor's voice. But then, I thought, she always sounds like that. The only time I had ever heard her speak in a truly feminine way was during her interview for the assistant medical examiner's position last year.

"I'll go get the nurse. He might need some more Demerol," Gus said compassionately as he turned and left the room.

"Mark, you have to tell me what happened," Karen demanded, leaning across the bed and inching closer to my face.

My memories of the shooting were slowly returning, but many of the details remained unclear. "Well, based on the injuries you've just outlined, I think it's safe to say I was shot."

"Don't be a smartass. Tell me something I don't know."

Karen had an engaging way of drifting into her own brand of cynicism when she was particularly annoyed. I always found it rather attractive since her demeanor was usually so formal and professional. Deciding to hedge the issue until I was more alert, I responded, "I don't think I'm ready to talk about what happened yet. I'm not really thinking too clearly."

Gus entered the room just in time with a nurse in tow.

Karen shot Gus a harsh look for the interruption and eased away from the bed. Obviously she wasn't through interrogating me. The nurse was carrying a syringe on a tray and asked me if I was ready for another shot.

"Sure. That sounds just like what the doctor ordered."

Karen studied her watch impatiently as the nurse finished her injection and started to leave.

"I have to get back to the office, Mark. There are three cases to do: the two bodies found near you on the pavement and then an older man who died suddenly, probably a heart case. We'll talk after you feel better, maybe tomorrow." She squeezed my good hand and abruptly marched out.

I looked at Gus quizzically, and he gave me a wink. Karen's officiousness didn't bother him in the least. One of the best detectives in the business, Gus was an excellent judge of character. He knew Karen's brusqueness was a front, probably because she was a woman on her own for the first time in a male-dominated profession. She put on the mask of a hard, strong woman in order to gain the respect she thought she deserved.

Gus retreated to the large stuffed chair in the corner of the room without saying a word. He unfolded his crumpled newspaper and took a sip of coffee from a stained paper cup he'd been carrying. I promptly fell asleep.

Gus was dozing off in the chair when I woke again. Within minutes, he too, opened his eyes and studied my face intently before offering me a glass of water. I drank it greedily. No natural light brightened the window, so I knew it must be late.

"Has Karen come by?" I asked.

"She looked in a little while ago, but couldn't stay long."

I knew Karen wouldn't dedicate much time to an incapacitated survivor. She was too compulsive and goal-oriented to waste time developing what she considered to be an unnecessary bedside manner. Gus was slouched in the same chair, absently thumbing through a magazine. I was still sore, but feeling much more alert.

"Don't you have some work to do?" I chided Gus. Genuinely concerned about how I was feeling, he seemed taken aback by my unsuccessful attempt at humor.

"Things are pretty well covered at the office. Karen, I mean Dr. Lipper, is doing a good job. Everything's under control." He waited, obviously hoping I was ready to talk. I definitely wasn't.

He continued on, "Sid Freeman was here after Karen. I was able to hold him off until you're more rested. I convinced him to come back in the morning."

"I appreciate that, Gus. I don't feel much like talking now."

"You'll have to talk to him sooner or later. He'll need to know what this incident was all about. He has lots of questions, and almost as many theories, about what must have happened. I guess we all have quite a few questions."

I smiled at his formality. Always courteous and respectful, Gus never seemed willing to transcend the imaginary barriers between employee and boss. I'd long since given up on breaking down his ingrained notions about how the hired help should act. As I searched his worried expression, I knew I owed him some sort of explanation, but reluctant to expose my own foolishness, I hesitated.

"Gus, I want and need to tell you everything that's happened, but my mind is still a little fuzzy. If you give me tonight to get my head clear, I'll go over everything with you in the morning."

It was almost time for the evening meal to be delivered to the room. I told Gus I wanted him to go home, eat, and get some rest, but he was reluctant to leave. He still thought I needed protection. In the morning he'd realize the danger for me was over. The man who had caused the recent hell in my life was dead. I'd sleep more comfortably tonight than I had in weeks.

"You sure?" he asked.

"Yes, I'm sure. I'll be safe."

Gus gave a slight nod, turned, and left.

A few more well-wishers came by after dinner. By 8:30 I was free to relive all that had happened to me within the last few months. Gus deserved the complete story. I wanted to remember everything in order to give him all the details, without leaving anything out.

GUS RETURNED AT EXACTLY 7:00 A.M. with a cup of steaming coffee in one hand a doughnut in the other. He assumed his usual position in the chair across from me. A nurse was taking my vital signs when he entered. I nodded to recognize him, and he returned a similar silent welcome.

When the nurse finished, I told Gus to slide his chair over next to the bed. I was prepared to recount the last few months of my life.

"You ready?" I asked.

"Sure. Fire away." He sipped some coffee with an expectant look on his face.

"Of course, Gus, you know this all happened because of you," I said, smiling.

"Me?" Gus responded with a look of bewilderment.

"Yeah. You stayed in San Diego at the forensic meeting with Karen, and I came home early. If you'd returned home instead of me, you'd probably be lying here in pain, and I'd be over there, lounging in a chair, eating and watching you suffer."

"How do you figure, Doc?" Gus asked.

"Oh, it's just another doomed attempt at humor. I'm the only person I know who could have been stupid enough to get embroiled in a mess like this. I totally lost my objectivity in the case I came home to."

"Now I'm completely confused. Maybe you better start back at the forensic meeting," Gus said, picking some doughnut crumbs off of his trousers.

2

I had arrived in San Diego the night before the first day of the meeting. The hour was late and I had gone to bed early.

I AWOKE FOR THE SECOND TIME that night. Sleeping in a hotel room had always been difficult for me. I guess I was just a creature of habit, too used to my own lumpy bed, my ancient pillow, and my familiar surroundings. Hotel rooms reminded me of the many crime scenes I'd surveyed over the years. I couldn't shake the feeling of vague uneasiness. Besides, my prostate rarely allowed me to make it through the night without the inevitable nuisance of a sense of urgency. At 47, I was rather exasperated to be experiencing the problems of an elderly man, but the annual finger prodding by my physician had failed to discover any abnormality or enlargement. Maybe my considerable coffee intake was to blame.

Now undeniably awake, I walked to the window and stared at the San Diego skyline from my 14th floor window. The city still slept, and it was too early to get up. The morning forensic conference was still hours away. I returned to bed, propped up a couple of pillows, turned on the bedside light, and grabbed one of my Louis L'Amour books. They were always my first choice for late-night reading because their simplistic plots didn't require any intellectual effort. I thumbed the pages to Chapter Two, but then my thoughts drifted.

I was in my 15th year as the Medical Examiner for Greene County. After my forensic training in New York City, I realized I couldn't ignore my rural roots. Returning to the Midwest was the only choice I could make. The big city grated on my nerves. The paranoia of the urban dwellers and their fast-paced lifestyle had become unbearable. I was more than ready to come back to the Midwest by the time my two years of training were complete. Working in Missouri was my childhood fantasy redesigned as reality. I'd always liked Springfield, the site of frequent family trips from our farm in the southwestern part of the state near Neosho.

I refocused on L'Amour and let his storytelling weave its magic. . . .

THE AUTOMATED WAKE-UP CALL startled me at 6:30 A.M. I slowly arose from bed and then remembered I was having breakfast with Gus. He had been my extended right hand for years. A retired detective from St. Louis, he knew how to investigate a case properly. I always found his directness refreshing.

He never minced words, and he had more integrity than anyone I knew. We had become that rare combination of colleagues who were also very good friends.

Gus wanted to meet me for bagels and coffee at 8:15. Then I had to meet Karen in front of the convention hall at 8:55. I had been asked to make some opening remarks and then introduce the plenary session speakers at 9:00, a job I hadn't agreed to do until Karen exerted considerable pressure. Because she was so persuasive, I found it difficult to say no.

I wasn't particularly excited about giving this talk. I hadn't participated in the Forensic Academy or published anything in years, although I had attended the last meeting in San Diego a few years ago. Some of the younger members of the association, including Karen, were trying to bring me back into the mainstream. I guess they thought I still had something to offer.

Earlier in my career, I'd published numerous articles and a couple of texts about forensic pathology. They had been well received, and I seemed to be a popular speaker who traveled the circuit teaching the importance of teamwork in death investigation. After a while though, I became bored with lecturing, and when my wife began complaining about the time I was spending away from her, it was easy to start saying no. Eventually I stopped taking part in meetings and giving lectures and decided to concentrate solely on my job in Springfield. For a while, I was asked to take part in seminars and other educational opportunities, but the calls quit coming when I never accepted.

At least my opening remarks hadn't taken much time to prepare. I was asked to speak for only 15 minutes, so I decided to adapt a lecture I had given 10 years ago that focused on cause and manner of death and a pathologist's limitations. It would fit right in with the Academy's attempt to develop cross-training among its varied members. Karen, however, couldn't believe I was going to use some old, faded slides as my visuals. Determined that most of the slides had to be updated, she made new ones with a snazzy PowerPoint program. She said she wasn't going to be embarrassed by my inherent laziness.

"You're too well-respected to show crap like that," Karen admonished.

My final act of preparation for the day's activities was to don the new floral tie Karen had given me in honor of the task at hand. I hadn't worn a tie since my wife divorced me almost three years ago. Even testifying in court wasn't reason enough to put my own neck in a stranglehold.

While shaving, I tried not to dwell on how old I was looking. The creases etched in my forehead and along the outside of my eyes seemed to be more pronounced since my divorce. I hurriedly finished shaving so the face in the mirror would go away. After my toiletries were completed, I dressed for the morning's event. The old suit I had brought along was another area of contention between Karen and me. She was appalled at its lack of style and the generally worn condition of the wool. But I refused to buy a suit for a single 15 minutes in the limelight. I avoided looking in the mirror and instead grabbed my slides and notes and headed out the door, determined to get this presentation over with.

LATER THAT AFTERNOON, I was relaxing in the hotel bar, rewarding myself for having survived another forensic presentation. I grabbed a handful of complimentary peanuts as I waved to the bartender for another drink. He remembered I had been drinking bourbon and quickly responded to my signal.

"Do you know what happened to a bartender named George who used to work here? I don't remember his last name. He was a short, stocky fellow, always full of jokes, " I inquired.

"That would be George Cunningham. He's been gone for over a year now. Left just after the bar was remodeled. Went up to Alaska, I think, to live with his brother."

I remembered George as a classic, old-time bartender who loved his work and cared about his customers. He'd been a memorable fixture, difficult to forget. George would not have approved of the new changes. While he had always been dressed neatly in a white shirt with a red bow tie, his new replacement peered out from under a ratty cowboy hat and tried to act comfortable in some very tight, faded jeans.

The owners of the bar had attempted to recreate a Western motif. They'd replaced the dark wood paneling and marble-topped bar with barn siding and a gaudy countertop complete with a fake leather arm-pad along the edge. There was similar upholstery on the chairs that encircled the wooden tables throughout the room. The finishing touch was an aging set of elk horns hanging over the mirror behind the bar. The bar had been renamed "The Watering Hole."

"I can understand why he left," I muttered as I looked around the bar. The bartender followed my glance, and then gazed at me blankly.

"When was the last time you were here?" he asked.

I pondered for a moment and then answered, "Three or four years ago, I think. I can't exactly remember when our group was here last."

"Oh, you're with the medical convention. You one of the Quincys?" The bartender clearly knew the convention center was holding the annual forensic meeting. What he knew about forensic pathology was probably limited to the old television series that made the job of medical examiners seem glorious and heroic.

"I guess so," I uttered with little enthusiasm.

Sensing no opportunity for conversation, the bartender sauntered over to the sink and resumed his task of washing an interminable stack of dirty glasses.

After another drink, I finally relaxed. My talk at the plenary session seemed to have gone well. Several members congratulated me at the end of the session, and even Karen gave me her nod of approval as she walked by with another colleague. I'd made a quick getaway and escaped to change clothes. A plaid shirt and wrinkled khaki trousers had been a welcome change from the scratchy, hot suit.

I grabbed the remaining peanuts in the bowl and washed them down with the last bit of bourbon in my glass. Withholding the urge to order another drink, I waved off the bartender who had noticed my empty glass.

A throng of conventioneers began pouring into the bar. The scientific sessions and the later business meetings I hadn't attended were finished for the day. Some of the attendees nodded when they recognized me as one of the plenary speakers. None of the faces were familiar until two old veterans entered and noticed me at the bar. They stopped by to congratulate me on my "insightful" comments delivered at the plenary session. Both said they hoped I would consider becoming more involved in future scientific programs. They felt that more of my experience was needed to lead the younger members of the society. After they walked away, I had to admit to myself that their words definitely made me feel good.

I thought about the increasing numbers of younger pathologists who needed some guidance. More and more pathologists were choosing forensic pathology, probably due to the increase in government control over other areas of pathology and medicine in general. I expected more physicians to either quit medicine as a profession or go into other fields where there was less bureaucracy. Even those pathologists who never liked to perform autopsies were coming back to the specialty of forensics. The pay wasn't as good as in private practice, but there were fewer problems with insurance and billing.

I overheard several people talking about some of the more intriguing papers they'd heard. Karen's name was mentioned more than once. She had presented a paper early in the afternoon. The comments were generally favorable.

"I thought I'd find you here."

I turned to see Karen pushing past two men in the doorway. Though obviously displeased at finding me in the bar, she attempted to mask her disapproval. She didn't care for drinkers. Something or someone associated with alcohol in her past had probably given her a bad time. I never pried, and she never volunteered an explanation. When she first came to work for me, she would unleash her venom on all the dead alcoholics who ended up on our morgue tables. Since the numbers kept mounting, she had a lot to say.

Karen grabbed my arm and started talking about her presentation. "Dr. Smithy ran the projector. What an ass! He kept adjusting each slide trying to get a better focus, but he made it worse. My slides were good, so I told him to relax and leave the projector alone. The audience applauded, and my case was so interesting no one paid much attention to him."

At one time, Karen's excessive boasting would have forced me to respond, but I let it go, accepting what I couldn't change. Karen was at that stage in her career when giving a presentation before the Academy was something special. I had long passed the need for fame and recognition in my own career.

I had to admit her case was a worthwhile one. Only a few similar cases had been reported. A man had died because of a fluid-filled cyst of the brain. Most pathologists, even experienced ones, would have missed it. But Karen detected it in a 26-year-old man who had been found dead by his wife after she came home from working the late shift at Denny's. I would have suspected congenital heart disease or an overdose as the cause. Yes, picking up the cyst was certainly perceptive.

"You think they minded you not having the actual photos of the brain?" I interrupted.

"No, not at all." She responded with confidence. "I had the illustrator draw the pictures so that the case would be both life-like and easy to understand because I knew not everyone in the room would be a pathologist. You could easily see on one slide the gelatinous, round, ball-like cyst suspended on a stock. Another slide showed how the cyst acted like a ball valve to close off the third ventricle in the brain. The last slide illustrated how the cyst plugged up the opening, causing an abrupt increase in brain pressure which rendered the decedent suddenly unconscious and finally dead." She caught her breath. "But of course you already know all this. I showed you the slides last week."

"No, I didn't see them." At least I didn't think I had, but I was becoming a little forgetful lately. Karen rarely came to me to share interesting cases or to ask for advice. We did go over a few of the most unusual cases together, but not many. While I left her free to do her share of the cases, I sometimes wondered if I should oversee her work more often.

"Oh well, enough of that. Let's go get something to eat," she gushed.

We rose to leave and as I turned, I almost knocked over an old friend. It was Elizabeth Demarco, the chief medical examiner for the state of Tennessee. I had always liked the way she looked: tall, with long dark hair and a well-toned body. She was a woman that many men, including myself, had fantasized about over the years.

"Well, Mark, I really enjoyed your talk this morning. Your presentation was the bright spot in an otherwise boring plenary session. I appreciate how you're able to present your ideas within a few minutes and not drag out the obvious. I've always been impressed with your work. The other speakers were so atrocious. I got up and left early because I couldn't take another minute."

"Thanks for the kind comments, Elizabeth. I don't hear that many anymore." She seemed far friendlier than I remembered. I decided to be spontaneous.

"Would you care to join us for dinner?" I didn't want to sit through dinner listening to more of Karen's endless chatter about her presentation.

"I couldn't impose."

"No imposition whatsoever. Isn't that right, Karen?"

Karen looked momentarily confused, but recovered quickly.

"Oh, you two go ahead. I promised Jim Sanderson I'd meet him in the other lounge. He wanted to talk to me about my presentation. He said he'd had a similar case last year and suggested we might be able to collaborate on a paper."

I accepted her skillful excuse at face value; Karen never relished playing second fiddle to any other woman.

"I'm sorry you won't be able to join us," Elizabeth said. Surprisingly, she didn't sound sorry in the least.

"We'd better hurry if we want to get a table. I'll see you later, Karen," I said.

Elizabeth and I wandered away in search of the nearest restaurant. The most telling comment of the evening was her next remark. "I know you've been in the bar for awhile, Mark, and you're way ahead of me. Let me catch up to you during dinner."

I wasn't going to argue with a comment like that. An unfamiliar sense of self-confidence began to force its way into my mind. I had expected to end up in the bar alone or with a few old friends if I could hook up with them. Being with Elizabeth was like finding an oasis in my desert of self-imposed isolation. We both agreed to try the revolving seafood restaurant on the top floor of the hotel.

Predictably, it was overpriced, overdecorated, and overrated. The so-called ambiance made us feel like we were part of the catch-of-the-day. But somehow it didn't seem to matter. Elizabeth and I slipped into a congenial, almost flirtatious relationship as we drank and talked for hours. After dinner we ended up back in the bar. By midnight, I had consumed too much alcohol, and I was exhausted. I decided to call it a night.

When I rose to leave, Elizabeth grabbed my arm and said

she wanted to do the same. I was slow to realize what she was suggesting. On the rebound from a recent divorce, she was obviously not concerned with emotional commitments or strings of any kind. I guessed I was the catch-of-the-day after all. When I told her I was tired and didn't know if I'd be up to her expectations, she responded, "No problem, Mark, I'll do all the work."

And she certainly did.

3

I flew out of San Diego the next morning, pleased that Gus and Karen could have an extra day or two before they had to get back to the grind. After arriving home, I spent the remainder of the day doing errands and going through the mail. Intent on spending a peaceful night asleep in my own lumpy but familiar bed, I was asleep by 9:00 P.M. without even picking up my Louis L'Amour.

The horn was just announcing the ship's arrival in port as I dreamed of lapping up a luxury cruise. The horn sounded twice before I became alert enough to realize with disappointment that the horn was the telephone ringing. I struggled to sit upright on the side of the bed, clearing my head before I answered.

"Hello," I barked. I wasn't used to such early calls sabotaging my sleep. Since Gus and then Karen had been hired, I hadn't taken any night calls, one of the perks of being chief.

"Dr. Jamison?" the 911 dispatcher asked.

"This is he," I grumbled, eyeballing 5:40 A.M. on the bedside clock.

"We've had a death over on Seventh and the officers would like you to respond."

For a moment I wondered why I was being called. But then I remembered that Gus and Karen had stayed an extra day in San Diego and I was on call.

"What do they have?"

"I'm not sure, but the body is in the front yard and they need you."

I recalled that the phone ringing in the middle of the night and the odd hours of the job were part of the reason my marriage had failed. I was rarely able to leave town because there was no other pathologist who could cover for me. But that all changed five years ago when I threatened to quit if the commission didn't agree to hire an investigator. Ten years of being on call, day in and day out, was enough. Then Gus miraculously appeared on the scene to save my professional life. Unfortunately it was too little, too late, to save my marriage.

Seventh Street, on the north side of town near the courthouse, was in an area of older homes built in the forties and fifties that had seen better days. As I turned my dilapidated Toyota onto Seventh, I saw the crowd gathered along both sides of the street. It always amazed me to see how many people were willing to get up before dawn to hang out at a crime scene. As I parked my car along the curb, I discerned the tall, slim figure of Sid Freeman heading towards me. An experienced detective, Sid was one of the few permanent fixtures in a department where most of the detectives rotated through the death investigation unit every six months. It was good to see a familiar face.

"Hi, Sid."

"We've got quite a mess here," Sid commented, with no introduction, pointing to a covered body on the sidewalk.

"What's going on?"

"There are parts of this man's face all over the place. We found pieces as far away as that porch across the street."

Sid waved towards the small, green, ramshackle house where a uniformed officer was standing on the porch.

"Well, let me see the body."

"It's over here."

We gingerly stepped over the pieces of tissue on the pavement to reach the body, lying on the sidewalk. It was covered with a flowered bedspread. I bent down and lifted the covering. The body was face down and blood was seeping from a facial wound onto the concrete. A double-barreled shotgun was lying next to the body. I looked from the body to Sid.

"He sure did a job on himself. Who is he?"

"His name is Joe Benton. He had a fight with his girlfriend last night and must have left the house with the gun while she was sleeping. She'd tried to take the gun away from him earlier in the evening, but obviously she wasn't successful."

"I can't really see much."

"Do you want us to roll him over?"

"Yes, I need to see the face better. Let's do it quickly and not make a big production out of this. I don't want all of these neighbors gawking if we can help it."

"I hear you." Sid grabbed a couple of patrolmen and told them to hold the bedspread around the body, shielding it from the curious onlookers. Sid and I awkwardly rolled the body over. It was a gruesome sight, especially the first thing in the morning. The shotgun blast had blown out most of the face from below the mouth to the eyebrows. A bloody hole filled with bits of bone and tissue is all that remained.

I lifted up the chin and could see a separate, roughly circular hole with blackened edges. I knew this must be the entrance wound. The gunpowder around the wound meant the gun had been very close or loosely touching the skin as it was fired. After seeing the gunpowder, I quickly flexed the decedent's jaw, elbows and knees before standing up.

"OK, Sid, I've seen enough. We can call the funeral home."

"Do you want him taken to the morgue first?"

"Yes, I'll take a closer look at him later this afternoon."

The detectives immediately drew the bedspread back over the body as Sid and I walked out into the street. We both noticed a pair of policemen, heads bent, studying the ground as they took note of the widely scattered fragments of the dead man's face. One of the men was writing as the other knelt down to get a better view of the evidence. Each of the pieces was resting on a sheet of white notebook paper. There must have been more than 100 sheets up and down the road. Unaware that we were within hearing distance, I heard one of the men loudly utter "hamburger." I thought I'd misunderstood until the word was distinctly repeated. I turned to Sid.

"Hell, what are these guys doing, Sid?"

He looked at me quizzically and said, "They're labeling the evidence."

"I know that's standard procedure, but this is a little different. These are pieces of a man's face. Who's the guy writing in the notebook?"

"That's Robert White. He's just out of the Academy and likes to do things by the book. We find it best just to leave him alone."

"Well, maybe you could get him to say anything but 'hamburger' as he's doing his recording. The neighbors relishing this process don't need to hear policemen describing pieces of a dead man's face as part of a lunch menu."

Sid approached the two men. I didn't overhear the conversation, but after a moment the men glanced my way and then immediately sobered up, adopting a much more professional-looking demeanor. Sid returned with a small smile playing about his lips and asked me to accompany him to the green house across the street. The patrolman guarding the front porch didn't respond as I nodded a greeting. Photographers from the local media were busily snapping photos as I crouched down to study the tissue on the uneven planks. It was a well-formed square of skin and hair, obviously part of the dead man's mustache and nose.

"Part of his nose?" queried Sid.

"Yes, it's from the left side of his face. See the edge of his upper lip? This is his mustache." I flipped the piece over with my pen for a more complete examination.

"Let's put this in a bag."

Sid nodded to the policeman who hurriedly left the porch and returned with a plastic bag and a pair of rubber gloves. He rolled his eyes in disgust as I declined the offer of the gloves, picked up the specimen between my fingers, and dropped it into the bag.

"Sid, do you have anything else for me to see?"

"No, I don't think so."

"Your officer looked a little squeamish back there," I remarked, heading back to the street.

"I know. It's all about AIDS. Everyone's so uptight about touching anything because they think they're going to catch it."

"There's no way he's going to get AIDS from picking up a piece of tissue like that."

"I know, I know. You've drilled that into me enough times, but some of the younger guys don't know or haven't gotten the message yet."

"Sid, are there any witnesses?"

"Just the girlfriend. She's in the house—kind of shook up, but she'll talk to you."

The cheap, metal door made the expected hollow retort as I knocked. I opened the door after a quiet invitation came from inside. Seated on a worn, overstuffed sofa was a tired-looking, very upset young woman. She was sobbing on the shoulder of a male companion. I introduced myself and was met with a look of derision by the man. What was his problem? I wasn't the bad guy here.

Once I had established that this young woman was the dead man's girlfriend, I began to try to figure out what had happened. Though she was clearly shaken, the woman agreeably answered all my questions. She recounted how her boyfriend had gotten "shit-faced" the night before and had wanted to fight Danny, the man whose shoulder she was currently using.

"Joe was angry because I was dancing with Danny up at the Roundhouse."

"I didn't do anything!" Danny seemed ready to explode and I felt oddly out of place in the midst of this jealous triangle. I wished Gus were here to take over; it was the kind of situation he seemed to enjoy.

"I'm not saying you did. I'm just trying to find out what happened."

The girl placed her hand on the man's leg to calm him down. I was impressed with her ability to keep Danny quiet and to tell her story even though she was still quite emotional. She had a quiet, unassuming intelligence that seemed sharply incongruous with this setting. The young woman continued her explanation.

"Joe and I began to argue as soon as I left the dance floor with Danny. He said the only way for a 'dumbshit' like Danny to get the message was to fire a few shots at him. I convinced Danny to leave the bar, and then I tried to settle Joe down, but he was still totally irrational. The bartender was pretty annoyed with all of us, and he sent a couple of his regulars to be sure Danny had left the premises. I corralled Joe, but he was determined to walk home, get his shotgun, and go after Danny."

"I walked back to the house with him, using everything I could think of to calm him, but he completely tuned me out. Once we were back here, he headed straight for his shotgun and his shells. I wrestled the shells away from him, but he wouldn't give up his gun. He spent most of the night pacing the floor and I eventually fell asleep on the sofa, feeling pretty secure that he couldn't do any real damage with an unloaded gun."

"Sometime in the early morning, he must have removed the shells from my lap while I was sleeping. I woke up when I heard the shotgun blast, and I called 911 right away. I still don't know why he killed himself—I thought he wanted to kill Danny! I was sure we could have talked things out when he was sober. There was no reason for him to blow himself away. Danny didn't mean anything to me at all. I just wanted to make Joe jealous so he'd pay more attention to me."

At this point her sobbing took over and she was back to relying on Danny's nearby shoulder. I wondered momentarily how Danny felt when she'd said he meant nothing to her at all. Realizing I didn't have any more questions, I went back outside to find Sid. He met me on the porch.

"That guy Danny give you any trouble?"

"Not really, but I felt like he was ready to lay into me if I did or said anything he didn't like. Why... who is he?"

"Just a jerk that's given us some trouble in the past. He's got a long sheet, but nothing too bad. He's really just a wimp with a big mouth. Likes to pick on women, usually very weak ones."

"Can't you get him on anything?"

"Nah. None of his lady friends will ever turn him in. Must be true love," Sid said sarcastically.

"I can add him to my growing list of stellar citizens," I muttered. Sid looked at me in agreement.

"I'll be looking at Joe sometime this afternoon. Do you want me to give you a call?"

"No thanks, I'll pass. Just let me know if you find anything unusual."

4

I took the freeway back to the office. I was traveling eastbound when I noticed the red lights of emergency vehicles in the westbound lane below the overpass. I instinctively slowed for a closer look and saw a large, white car smashed against the bridge abutment. The next exit was just ahead so I pulled off and headed back.

The traffic was congested and almost stopped as I worked my way around the lines of impatient motorists and onto the shoulder. A frenzied policeman began waving his arms as he headed toward me, obviously upset that I was driving on the shoulder. He was still incensed as I stopped my car in front of him. After I gave him my name, he calmed down considerably, although his face was still flushed and perspiring. He curtly commanded me to park behind the last emergency vehicle in the line.

Firemen were shielding the driver's side of the damaged vehicle with a blanket as I approached the scene.

The first thing I noticed about the car was the vanity license tag that read "DRBONES." I was generally perturbed when doctors flaunted their specialties like this. The public already considered most doctors to be overly pompous and arrogant. My thoughts drifted to what kind of obnoxious tag I could come up with for myself. Possibly "Dr. Death" or "Meatman" might be appropriate. I was thinking of other possibilities when I suddenly realized that I'd seen this license plate before. The big white Cadillac was also familiar, but I couldn't place the owner in my mind.

Sgt. Patterson of the traffic unit saw me and walked over.

"Good morning, Doc. How'd you get here so soon? I just called your office a minute ago."

"Hi, Jim. I happened to be driving by on my way home from another scene."

"I heard about that one down at the station—sounds like the guy's face was really a mess."

"He certainly wasn't much to look at. Who do we have in the car?"

"His name is Dr. John Thomas. No skid marks, but I don't think it was a suicide. Maybe he had a heart attack. Doc, is something wrong?"

Jim must have noticed that the name had made an impression on me. I suppose these detectives were amazed whenever I showed any emotion because I usually tried to stay very cool and dispassionate.

"I'm all right. I know the man . . . well, not him . . . but his wife."

"I should have guessed. He is a doctor. You probably know all the docs in town."

The two of us walked over to the firemen holding the blanket. Once again Jim began reciting possible theories for the cause of the accident.

"It's almost like Dr. Thomas headed for the bridge on purpose because we'd see some skid marks if he'd tried to put on his brakes. But why would a guy like him want to commit suicide? Maybe he reached over for something on the floor of the car and then just lost control. I doubt he would fall asleep at the wheel this early in the morning."

I looked into the car while Sgt. Patterson continued his rambling. Dr. Thomas was slumped over onto the passenger side of the front seat. The airbag had deployed and was lying deflated over his legs. Though rumpled, the man's expensively tailored suit was clean and blood-free. Papers were strewn about the front seat, and a broken coffee cup was visible on the floor of the passenger side.

"It's too bad the bag didn't help him. Most people think it's impossible to die with one of those, but here's proof that even airbags aren't a sure thing. I'll bet he's torn up on the inside though."

Jim kept talking aloud, discussing the possible internal injuries the victim might have, most of it gleaned from what I had taught him in the past. He was right in thinking that I'd undoubtedly find a torn aorta or heart but minimal head trauma during the autopsy.

I made some mental notes of what I'd seen. There were

some scrapes on Dr. Thomas' hands and face. Nothing appeared unusual or especially significant at the scene. Before airbags, accidents such as these would cause tremendous external injuries, especially to the head and chest. Blood would usually be found splattered all over the inside of the vehicle. But airbags made the scenes cleaner. Head injuries from impacts against the front windshield were rare. Except for a few scrapes on the extremities, most injuries occurred on the inside of the body, usually to the major organs.

My thoughts shifted to Mary, the dead man's wife. I hadn't seen her for many years. We'd lived together in college and I'd assumed we'd eventually marry. Mary had studied abroad her junior year and although we promised to write and resume our relationship when she returned, she felt we had grown too far apart. We tried to pick up where we'd left off when she came back to school, but the chemistry wasn't there, especially from her perspective, and we had gone our separate ways. I had been hurt when she left, but some of my feelings for her had always remained with me.

I didn't hear all of what Jim was saying because I began thinking about the difficult task that lay ahead. I should be the one to notify Mary that her husband was dead. I hadn't done much death notification recently because Gus or the police usually took care of it. Throughout the years, I'd talked to scores of families, and I'd adopted a formula that helped me remain objective and professional. But never before had I needed to inform someone I was once in love with about a death. This was definitely not something I was eager to do. I surveyed the scene of the accident again and then turned to leave.

"Are you going to be doing this autopsy?" asked Jim.

"I'll do it later today," I answered reluctantly.

"Please give me a call. I'd like to watch if it's okay."

"Sure, it'll probably be after lunch. Since I know the decedent's wife, I'll go ahead and call her about her husband's accident."

"Thanks, Doc. I'll see you later."

I returned to my car, lost in thought. Somehow I automatically knew the way to Mary's house.

MY OLD TOYOTA was definitely out of place in this part of town. The mansions were hidden behind brick walls, guarding themselves from the less fortunate, but the manicured lawns were visible through the gates that spoke of private gardeners. Number 1305 was Mary's. The gate was open and I pulled into the drive. I kept waiting for security guards to rush my car and ask me what I was doing, but there were none. The narrow, asphalt drive led to a circle in front of a remarkable, two-story brick mansion with white columns. I slowed the car ever so slightly to lengthen the time I could gaze upon this almost perfect setting. But then I realized I had to deal with the problem at hand.

Standing before the ornate, inlaid wooden door, I experienced a mixture of feelings. I was excited to see Mary once again even though I was the bearer of such bad tidings. If I were being honest, I'd admit I'd always carried a torch for her. There were a few years during my marriage when I hadn't thought of her, but after my divorce I spent lots of time thinking of the past and the years we'd spent together. The memories seemed especially vivid now.

I lifted the massive brass knocker and let it fall. A few seconds passed before the door opened. A young man in his twenties with long, dark hair stood before me, eyeing me suspiciously.

"May I help you?" The young man's voice was cool, if not slightly hostile.

"I'm Dr. Jamison. Is Mary Thomas home? I need to speak to her."

"My mother isn't dressed. Maybe I could help."

"It is important that I speak to your mother." I recognized Mary's limpid blue eyes in the young man's face. He was obviously her son. He called up to his mother that she had company and then opened the door wide enough to allow me entrance.

I stepped into the foyer as he closed the door behind me and then quietly disappeared. I found myself standing on gleaming, forest-colored marble. On one side of the foyer was a stone facade with plants mysteriously growing out of the rock. Water trickled down the craggy surface of the wall into a pool filled with goldfish. Along the other side was a curved oak stairwell. I had never been in such an opulent home before. It was both impressive and overwhelming. I knew Mary had done well when she married an orthopedic surgeon, but I never thought about what kind of wealth this actually meant.

I glanced up to the top of the stairs and realized Mary was staring at me. She was dressed in a full-length, flowing robe. I could see that her dark hair was twisted about her head, but I couldn't make out her facial features easily until she began descending the stairs. I moved a few steps forward and then stopped when she spoke.

"Is that you, Mark? It's been so long. Why ever are you here?"

I didn't hear any of Mary's questions because I was totally immersed in her face. The years had changed her little. There were a few fine wrinkles around her eyes and mouth, but these seemed to add to her overall look of mature sophistication. Her flawless white smile was welcoming, and her skin held the glow of careful tanning and meticulous moisturizing. But it was the eyes that pulled me in. They were the same transparent, sky blue that I remembered, incredibly seductive and beguiling. Realizing I was staring, I shifted my glance uncomfortably.

"Mark," she spoke again firmly, bringing me back to the task at hand.

"Oh yes, I'm sorry," I responded awkwardly.

"Why are you here?"

"I need to talk to you about John."

"What about John? What's wrong with him?"

Most people suspect the worst when a member of law enforcement or a death investigator arrives on the doorstep. Mary knew enough of my occupation to naturally assume the worst. I fumbled for a response.

"Let's go sit down, Mark." I discerned the familiar terror in her eyes that I'd seen in countless faces before. She led me directly into a room to the right of the stairwell, and I followed hesitantly. She motioned me into one of the plush, red leather chairs artfully arranged in the center of what was obviously a library or study. I perched tensely on the edge of the cushion, clearly at a loss for a way to begin.

Mary rescued me. "He's dead, isn't he?" The tears began to form in the inner corners of both eyes, but she maintained a very regal posture.

I couldn't seem to get any words out.

"Mark, please, can you tell me what happened?"

"His car ran into the bridge abutment at the Division St.

exit on 65. There were no skid marks. His airbag deployed, but the impact must have been so great that he couldn't survive." I spontaneously decided to postpone further details until I was absolutely sure of the cause of death.

"Why did it happen?" she asked quietly, with unwavering eye contact.

"I'm not sure. I'll know more after the autopsy."

"Autopsy. Why do you have to do that?"

"An autopsy will help me understand exactly how he died."

"But why? Didn't he die in the accident?"

"I'm sure he did. I just need to be totally sure."

"I know he wouldn't have wanted one," she responded quickly.

Sensing her obvious discomfort, I attempted to calm her down.

"Mary." Saying her name out loud for the first time in 20 years seemed strange. "I perform autopsies on all drivers in motor vehicle accidents when I'm not 100 percent sure of either the cause of the accident or the cause of the person's death. There's nothing unusual in this."

"But I know he wouldn't have wanted one," she repeated.

I felt reluctant to force the standard protocol on her, but I could only reiterate my professional requirements for cases like this one.

"I wish I could avoid an autopsy, Mary, but I can't. We have to rule out any suspicion of foul play or wrongdoing. I'm a public official and this is just part of my job." I sounded a little too officious, but I didn't know any other approach to take.

Mary slumped back against the chair back, obviously accepting my resolute attitude as unequivocal.

"I understand, Mark. When will the autopsy be complete?"

I felt I owed Mary the best possible autopsy, and I wanted to be sure every detail concerning the case was covered. Karen would probably question the ethics of my performing an autopsy on someone I knew, but I was also aware that Mary might feel more comfortable knowing the person who was going to be cutting on her dead husband.

"I can't give you an exact time, but it will be sometime this afternoon." I had this compelling urge to walk over to Mary's chair to comfort her, but I didn't. Showing affection wasn't one of my strong points. This was yet another of the many reasons why my marriage hadn't lasted. I stood up when Mary rose. She appeared to be struggling valiantly to maintain her composure.

"Mark, thank you for coming. I've always worried about some stranger giving me this kind of news. I am glad it was you."

I felt as though there must be something I should do at this point, but I didn't know what it was. So I turned, walked out of the room, and let myself out the front door. As I started the car and looked toward the house, I could see Mary watching me through the heavily curtained library window.

5

Bill Archer, the morgue attendant, was seated behind the desk perusing the sports page as I entered the room. A handsome African-American in his mid twenties who'd worked in the morgue for the past six months, he had replaced a man that I had worked with for over 15 years. Bill wasn't as skilled as his predecessor yet, but he had potential. He was a hard worker and willing to learn.

Bill had already placed the body of Dr. Thomas on the disinfected, stainless table. I carefully scrutinized the face of death. He didn't look the same as I remembered him, but then very few bodies ever resembled the people they had once been. I had viewed the remains of many acquaintances, especially women, whose faces and bodies bore few reminders of the beauty they had once possessed in life.

"He sure doesn't look like he was in a traffic accident," Bill commented. "Nothing wrong that I can see."

"His airbag prevented any external injuries, but you should have seen the damage to the car. He must have been going pretty fast the way he destroyed the front end."

"I thought airbags were supposed to save lives," muttered Bill.

"They usually do, but not if you're going too fast. A sudden stop can cause incredible damage inside your body while leaving few signs of injuries on the outside."

"Oh, I almost forgot. Sgt. Patterson called and said he wouldn't be able to make it. Something about another accident."

"Thanks for letting me know. We might as well get started then."

I examined the entire body carefully, making sure I didn't miss any injuries. Then I measured his length and made note of hair color, the absence of scars, tattoos or other abnormalities and checked the mouth. I dictated these findings into my hand-held recorder. Dr. Thomas, I thought, appeared to be sleeping peacefully more than he seemed dead.

Finished with the external examination, I proceeded to check for internal injuries. If the body was intact, I always followed the same procedure. I began the Y-shaped incision at each shoulder, joined it over the middle of the chest, and then continued in a straight line down the chest, over the abdomen adjacent to the belly button, and then to the pubic bone just above the genitals. Because I'd made these same cuts thousands of times before, my hands seemed to move on autopilot.

"I don't see any bleeding in the chest muscles at all," remarked Bill, as I reflected the skin away from the chest.

"No, but then I wouldn't expect to see much because the airbag distributes its force widely over the chest. We should see some injuries around the heart, though."

Next, Bill handed me the oscillating saw to cut through the ribs. I couldn't imagine how difficult this part might be without the modern technology of the saw. Its high-pitched, vibrating blade performed the job neatly and efficiently. I removed the chest plate, including the ribs, muscle and sternum, to expose the lungs, diaphragm and the sac that surrounded the heart. There was no blood around the lungs, in the chest cavities, or around the heart.

Without comment, I cut into the heart to retrieve a few tubes of blood for toxicological analysis and then removed the heart. I always preferred removing all the organs personally rather than having the morgue attendant do it because the feel of each organ added to my understanding of any abnormalities. Besides, the hands-on part of my job was really the aspect that I found to be most satisfying. It was the paperwork, budgets, and dependency on others that took some of the enjoyment out of forensic pathology.

After removing all the organs I examined the heart, paying particular attention to the aorta, the largest, most important blood vessel because it carries the blood from the heart to the rest of the body.

"Look at this."

Bill bent over to look at the tear in the aorta. "Yeah, I've seen that before." Bill didn't seem very impressed. "Not much blood."

"No, I'd expect more. In frontal impacts, the heart and aorta continue to travel forward during the sudden stop. The aorta tears just below the left subclavian artery that feeds blood to the arm. It's strange that there is so little blood in the tissues around the tear."

With few injuries and little blood in the tissues, I wasn't seeing what I'd anticipated. One of the basic rules in traffic accident fatalities is the expectation of bleeding in the tissues if someone was alive at the time of the accident. I wondered if Dr. Thomas could have been dead or dying at the moment of impact. I remembered the absence of skid marks at the scene. Maybe he was in the process of dying and couldn't apply the brakes.

The remainder of the abdominal exam was unrevealing. There were no signs of injuries to the stomach, liver, pancreas, kidneys or pelvic organs because the force of the impact was on the chest, not the abdomen.

"Bill, you can open the head while I finish up here."

"Sure."

Bill moved to the end of the table, picked up the scalpel, and began his work. He had to make the incision across the head a little lower because Dr. Thomas was slightly bald.

"Bill, make sure to cut back far enough. We don't want anyone seeing the sutures while he's in the casket."

"Of course, Doc. I know what to do."

"Sorry. I know his wife. I guess I'm being overly cautious.

Bill finished the incision and peeled the scalp away from the skull in preparation for the saw.

The saw's whirring resonated throughout the room until the skullcap was removed. The top of the brain was now exposed for examination.

"You want me to take the brain out?" inquired Bill, as I finished removing the abdominal organs.

"Do you see anything?"

"No blood, just a brain."

I glanced over to the head to where Bill was working and could see no blood over the surfaces of the brain. I had already viewed the undersurface of the scalp to look for bruises, but saw none, indicating no trauma.

"Go ahead and take it out."

While Bill was removing the brain, I weighed and began slicing the individual organs. Except for a few areas of blood in the lungs, I found little worth mentioning in any of the organs, including the brain that Bill had just handed me. I saved the heart to examine last. I usually did this since most adults have some heart disease, and I liked to finish an autopsy with some kind of positive finding if everything else has been negative.

I finally found the answer to the small amount of injury and blood inside the body. Dr. Thomas's heart weighed 550 grams, almost 150 grams more than I would anticipate in a 50-year-old man. His heart was definitely larger than the size of his fist, the normal size for an adult. The four chambers of his heart were expanded, indicating a heart that was beginning to fail. I began cutting the blood vessels which feed blood to the heart's wall. I discovered that many areas in the arteries were narrowed due to a buildup of fat and cholesterol.

"Look, Bill, he has some bad atherosclerosis."

"Huh? Oh yeah, that's hardening of the arteries, right?"

"Sure is. I'll bet the blood needed to feed oxygen to the heart just couldn't get through these clogged-up arteries. Some of these arteries are narrowed by almost 90 percent."

Bill was watching me making cuts through the heart's walls.

"Those walls look thick," he commented.

"They are. He must have had some high blood pressure

besides the diseased arteries. Look at this."

I pointed to at least two areas of white scarring in the wall that indicated old heart attacks. Was there any history of heart attacks? Of course I didn't know because I'd failed to ask Mary about her husband's past medical history. Usually I was compulsive about discovering the decedent's personal and medical history, but I'd become so caught up in the unusual circumstances of this case, I'd failed to follow my usual interviewing techniques. It was disquieting to realize how muddled I must have been during my meeting with Mary.

"Did he die of his heart disease or the accident?" Bill interrupted my thoughts.

"It looks like his heart disease got him. I would have expected a lot more internal bleeding if he had died as a result of the accident. The absence of blood suggests he was dead or dying before the impact. He certainly had a bad heart. This case is a little unusual in that most people having a heart attack while driving can pull off the road before they do much damage to the vehicle."

"He sure didn't have much bleeding, though."

I agreed but didn't answer. My initial evaluation was that Dr. Thomas had a heart attack or an arrhythmia, causing the heart to malfunction. The onset of a sudden arrhythmia causing a quick death might explain why he hadn't had time to stop the car. I still wanted to wait for toxicological testing to make sure I was comfortable with heart disease as a cause of death. I collected some urine, in addition to the blood I had already collected to send to the lab for a drug screen. Bill was removing the body from the table as I left the room to use the phone. I dialed Mary's number.

"Thomas residence," a formal voice answered.

"This is Dr. Jamison. Is Mrs. Thomas in?"

"I don't think I should disturb her at this time. Dr. Thomas died this morning, and I'm answering the phone for her."

"I know. I performed the autopsy and need to tell her the results."

"Oh, I'll see if she's available."

Mary's voice immediately came on the line. "Mark, this is Mary."

"Mary, I'm sorry to bother you, but I wanted to tell you about John."

"Yes, I'm ready."

"John had a bad heart. His coronary arteries were pretty much plugged up. There were signs that he'd had at least two old heart attacks."

"Did a heart attack cause his accident?" she asked.

"I think so." I could have explained that his heart might just as easily have begun to have an abnormal rhythm without a heart attack, but I didn't think going over the causes of sudden death was necessary at this time.

"So his heart started to act up before he hit the bridge?"

"Yes.

"I don't think I understand. He didn't die because of the accident?"

"Probably not, but I have to wait until the tox report comes back before I can make a final ruling," I explained.

"The tox report?"

"I'm sorry. The toxicology report. The results of a drug screen."

There was a pause before Mary responded. "Are you suggesting he might have had some drugs in his system?"

"No, I'm not implying anything of the sort. This is purely routine. I have drug screens done on all cases." I attempted to reassure her that I didn't really think there would be any illicit drugs in his system.

"Mark, I don't know if I understand all of this now. Do you think I could talk to you about this later? Could you call me after the funeral?"

"Of course. When is the funeral?"

"I'm not sure yet. The people from the funeral home are here now. I can let you know."

"Mary, I'm so sorry for your loss." I hung up the phone. The statement seemed perfunctory and impersonal, but my repertoire of responses to death was woefully inadequate. I wished I had some magical words that could assuage her grief like a drug can ease a person's pain.

"Hey, Doc. The other body is on the table." My thoughts were once again disturbed as Bill yelled from the other room. "This one shouldn't take long. Damn, what a job he did on his face." Bill was expounding on the remains of the man from this morning who had blown his face away with the shotgun.

"No, there doesn't seem to be much left of his face," I agreed.

I expected to see little pathology of the internal organs and I was right: all the organs were healthy. I collected some blood and urine for a drug screen, and then moved on to the head. Part of the man's brain was destroyed by the blast, and the face was almost totally obliterated. Out of habit I went looking for the morgue camera. Pictures of his face would be excellent illustrations of the effects of a close-up shotgun blast. I took a few photos of the entrance defect, both before and after Bill cleaned the face. I didn't teach much these days but something in me wanted to make a permanent visual record of unique cases. Over the years my collection had continued to grow even though I didn't show them to anyone.

I had noticed at the scene that the entrance wound under the chin was approximately one inch in diameter. The gunpowder on the edges of the wound proved the shotgun had been held close to the skin when it was fired. I did make an attempt to pull some of the edges of the facial defect together for another photo, but because so much of it was missing, I decided it wasn't worth the effort.

"Time for the head now?" Bill queried. Without waiting for my answer, he proceeded.

Bill didn't have to use the saw much because of the extensive fractures. After he cleared the way, I removed the brain and examined what was left. The main charge of the shotgun blast had torn away most of the brain's frontal lobes while the rest was relatively intact. Most of the shotgun pellets had exited the face, but I wanted to find a few of the 20 or so visible on x-ray to send to the lab. I mashed through some of the pulpified frontal area and came up with about 10 pellets. The lab liked to have at least 10 pellets to weigh and examine in order to determine the size of the shot. There were lead marks on the inside of some of the cranium where the pellets had struck the bone.

The case was a straightforward suicide, and after dictating the findings, I told Bill I was finished for the day, changed clothes, and left for home.

THE BARKING DOGS were a nuisance, but they had kept me company since the divorce. The twins were a pair of German Shepherds I inherited from my wife who wanted nothing more to do with them as she ventured into her new life. At first, I resented Millie shackling me with the raucous canines, but I forgave her long ago, after the dogs and I had become such good friends. Their constant barking was the only negative part of our relationship. Mortimer and Sleuth heard my car long before I squeezed the garage door opener. By the time I opened the door from the garage to the house, the dogs were absolutely out of control.

Mort leaped into the air and thumped his gigantic paws against my chest as I stepped through the doorway. He was a huge, purebred male, almost 100 pounds and by far the more aggressive of the two.

"Get down, you fool dog. You're going to ruin my clothes."

Sleuth whipped her tail back and forth against my trousers until I managed to disentangle myself from Mort long enough to give her some much-needed attention.

The dogs' frenetic energy slowed as I let them out into the backyard to eliminate their morning food and water. I prepared their evening meal and let them back inside. Once their heads were buried ravenously in their bowls, I escaped to the bedroom to shower and change my clothes.

The phone began to ring as I was rinsing the soap from my hair. Cursing, I flung open the shower door, grabbed a towel, and dripped my way over to the phone, leaving sopping footprints imprinted in the old shag carpet.

"Hi, Mark. It's me, Karen. I just wanted to let you know I'm back."

"Oh, hi. I didn't expect you until later."

"I told you Gus and I'd be back this evening. We really enjoyed the rest of the conference. I appreciate your taking call so we could stay the extra day. Have you had any interesting cases?"

"I had two today. One traffic and the other a suicide by shotgun. The guy blew some of his face across the street onto a neighbor's porch. You should have seen the look on the lady's face when she saw part of the dead man's mustache."

"That's disgusting," she responded.

As usual, she failed to see the humor in the situation. I'd always thought that without a relatively easy-going, jovial attitude about the steady stream of gruesome deaths and wasted lives I faced everyday, I'd end up totally crazy or at least in some sort of severe depression. Humor was the best method I'd found for maintaining a positive perspective.

"I guess you had to be there," was all I could say.

"Anything unusual about the traffic?"

"Not really. The man hit a bridge abutment. He was a doctor, an orthopod, and I know his wife."

"Anyone I know?" Karen asked.

"The name is Thomas."

"I recognize that name. I think my parents knew him."

Karen's parents knew Dr. Thomas. That made me feel much too old.

6

Because I was such a creature of habit, my daily routine was always the same. I walked the dogs after feeding them. Then I showered, shaved, and drank some orange juice before heading off to work. I stopped by the deli around the corner from the office and bought a plain, toasted bagel with a side order of butter. Freshly brewed coffee, prepared by Shirley Sweeney, my administrative assistant who had mothered me for years, awaited me at the office.

I hung up my coat and exchanged my morning greetings with Shirley who was already at work behind her desk. Even though we didn't talk very much, we understood each other. She knew how I thought the office and the business should be run. Because of her efforts, my job was easier and the business details were efficiently managed without causing me any additional stress.

In my office, I settled into my well-worn leather chair to eat my bagel and have my first jolt of caffeine. I was just getting ready to take a bite of my bagel, warm from being wrapped in foil, when Shirley rang me. She knew I generally needed a little time before dealing with phone calls and facing all the problems of the day, but Gus was on the line, so I knew it was important

"Chief, are you busy?" Gus asked.

"No, Gus. What do you need?"

"I'm over on Aztec Drive. You might want to come and see this one."

"What is it?"

"It's a surprise."

"I can hardly wait. Is this an emergency or can I finish my breakfast?"

"Take your time. I'll still be here when you arrive. You might want to bring Dr. Lipper with you. This one will blow her away! Let me tell you how to get here."

After Gus gave me the instructions, I decided to leave for the scene and finish my bagel en route. Gus rarely asked me to come to a scene unless he thought it an unusual one. He and I shared the same enthusiasm for extraordinary cases. I grabbed my coat and by the time I arrived downstairs at the morgue, I had devoured most of the remnants of the bagel. My mouth was still full when I found Karen bent over a table, cutting brains. She saw me come in and muttered a good morning. After swallowing the last of the bagel, I returned her terse greeting.

"Anything interesting?"

"Not much." She pointed to a brain she had already sliced up. "This one had a stroke, a good-sized one. Most of the left side of the brain was dead. After I fix the brain in formalin and let it sit for a week or so, the differences between the damaged and the normal areas should be even more obvious."

I nodded in agreement, and then said, "Gus just called to invite us to a scene. He's keeping the details quiet, so it must be pretty intriguing."

"Well, I am in the middle of something." She sounded exasperated at the interruption.

"Oh, come on. It might be worth your while, you never know."

She dropped her knife on the table. "At least let me wash my hands."

I could tell she wasn't in a very good mood so I didn't try to be my usual witty self. Karen flung her coat over her arm and we walked out to the parking lot. She wanted to drive and I acquiesced, giving her Gus's careful instructions. We found the house, a typical rental unit filled with students, about a half-mile from the university. The paint was peeling from the walls and a few shutters hung rakishly from the windows. Not surprisingly, the yard was littered with empty beer bottles and crumpled bags from McDonald's.

As I exited the passenger side of the car, I stepped directly into a puddle of water. I looked down at my sodden trouser leg, cursing my stupidity. I hoped no one had noticed, but when I looked up I saw Karen smirking. She rolled her eyes in disbelief of my clumsiness.

Approaching the front door, we were met by Sgt. Kennett,

one of Springfield's veteran detectives. He flung the screen door open for us.

"Looks like you had a little accident there, Doc. Well, at least you only have one trouser leg to be cleaned." Sgt. Kennett was known for his sarcastic humor that I usually enjoyed.

Without dwelling on the subject, I asked, "What do you have for us today?"

"You're going to like this one. Go see for yourself. First door on the right. Excuse me, good morning, Dr. Lipper." Sgt. Kennett wasn't as comfortable with Karen as he was with me.

More beer bottles, dirty dishes, and old newspapers were strewn about the front room. A guitar case was leaning against one wall and a set of drums stood guard in the corner. The only order to the room was the stereo with CDs lining the bookshelf. We met Gus in the hallway, exiting the first door on the right.

"I hope I didn't interrupt anything important. I thought you'd like to take a look at this one."

"No problem," I answered.

"Someone's been dead for awhile," Karen uttered as we both noticed the stench emanating from the open doorway.

Gus pushed the door open farther for us to see Pete Handler, one of the police department's younger crime scene technicians, perched in the middle of the bed. Various ropes, magazines, tapes, photographs, and reels of movie films covered the rumpled bedspread.

"Hi, Doc," Pete said as he lifted his Nikon to take another shot.

"Don't fall off there or I'll have more work on my hands," I chided. "Look at all this paraphernalia. Someone could open their own adult bookstore." My eyes shifted from one photo to another, taking in the varied array of couples engaged in every manner and position of sexual intercourse, as well as homosexual acrobatics. There were even a few selected shots of humans and animals. Some of the magazines graphically revealed a bound or gagged human being in the process of being whipped or tortured.

"Isn't this job great?" I asked Gus sardonically with a grin on my face, not expecting an answer.

Karen looked at me in disgust.

Propped against the bed was a full-length mirror, positioned to reflect the open closet. I focused on the mirror's image and then raised my eyes to the closet. The nude body of a young man was hanging from the closet rod. There was a rope around his neck that joined another which looped around his waist and went under his buttocks like a seat. A folded towel was haphazardly wrapped around his neck, but the rope had slipped under it and was pressing against the skin. It only took me a few seconds to realize that this was not a suicide.

"What do you think of this, Karen?"

"I've never seen one quite like this, but it looks like a sexual asphyxiation."

"Good. This is probably the best example of one I've ever seen."

"Isn't this a suicide?" Pete queried from atop the bed.

"No, this is an accidental death. The man didn't mean to kill himself."

"What was he trying to do?"

"He was masturbating."

Completely dumbfounded, Pete continued, "You mean

this guy was doing his thing while hanging there? Why would he want to do that?"

"From what I understand, if you constrict the flow of blood to the brain while you masturbate, then the orgasm is more intense. I've only heard this to be true. I don't have any first-hand experience," I joked.

Karen gave me an "Oh, please" look. Gus chuckled quietly.

"Why the towel?" Pete asked.

"I guess he didn't want to leave any marks on his neck. People might ask questions and it could be a little embarrassing if he engaged in this activity frequently. Are you using color film?"

"Sure."

"Would you mind making a set for me?" This was an exceptionally fine example of an autoerotic death and I wanted to have a complete record of it in my files.

"Be glad to." Pete didn't mind making copies or taking a few extra shots for me, probably because I rarely asked for anything that wasn't important. He climbed down off the bed, not easy to do gracefully for a man close to 300 pounds, and fished another lens from his camera bag.

"I'll get some good overalls and then some close-ups for you."

"Thanks, Pete."

I began to run through my normal mental routine. This was a young, white man in his twenties who was approximately 165 pounds and had shoulder length, black hair. A quick visual survey revealed there were no external injuries. I didn't expect to find any, but I still had to look to make sure nothing suspicious had happened. The lower part of the arms were a dark purple, signifying the blood had settled towards the floor due to the body's hanging position. There was a trickle of blood on the left side of the chin running from the mouth, a common finding in a hanging victim. Signs of decomposition were evident in the green discoloration of the skin and the bloating process that had already begun. No wonder the smell was so atrocious.

Gus, Karen, and I carefully studied the complicated course of the rope on the body. It was looped over one of two rods in the closet, the one above the wooden shelf. It hung to the man's neck where it was wrapped once around the towel and then continued down through the cleft of the buttocks. The rope was brought under the body between the testicles and the engorged penis, back up to the neck, and finally around the front of the body where it was tied in a slipknot after encircling the waist.

We discussed how the weight of the man's body had put too much pressure on the knot, making the slipknot escape route difficult to access when the young man began to lose consciousness.

"I guess the slip knot doesn't always work," Karen remarked dryly.

"Especially if you're unconscious," I answered.

I grabbed a chair and placed it next to the body. I climbed onto it and inspected the top of the closet. The edge of the shelf was quite worn. The decedent had undoubtedly participated in this activity numerous times before.

"Karen, take a look at this edge," I directed as I stepped off the chair.

Karen took my place on the chair and also felt the worn edge.

"I guess he's done this a few times before."

"They usually do it more than once," I replied. I noticed out of the corner of my eye that Pete was intently studying Karen's legs, a fact I hoped she wouldn't notice because I knew she could make quite a scene. I asked Gus if the decedent's identity was known.

"Yes, his name is Robert Smithton. He's lived here for over a year and a half with three other guys. They're all musicians. Most have part-time jobs, but Robert hasn't had one for a few months. We know he has a girlfriend. No one had seen him for a few days.

"He's got a girlfriend!" Karen exclaimed. "That doesn't make sense."

"You never know what we men are capable of doing," I kidded.

Predictably, Karen wasn't amused.

"The girlfriend doesn't understand why he would have killed himself," Gus chimed in. "I haven't told her exactly how he died except to say he was found hanging in the closest. I thought I would leave that job to one of you."

"Oh, thanks," I responded.

"I'd be glad to talk to her if you'd like," Karen offered. "I can't believe he would do this if he had a girlfriend."

"Be my guest."

Karen left to speak to the girlfriend who was sitting in the kitchen with a couple of the roommates. Gus asked me if I needed to see anything else and if there was going to be an autopsy.

"Not unless you think one is necessary," I answered.

DEADLY DECEIT

"No, we're sure how he died. I did find his address book and his mother's number. I'll give her a call."

"Gus, be careful how you handle this one. I don't think you need to be too explicit," I advised. "You can tell his mother the truth without giving too many unnecessary details about his sexual proclivities."

"Don't worry. I'll make it as easy on her as I can."

Until Karen returned, I strolled around for a few minutes, astonished at the quantity of the pornography amassed in one room.

"How did it go?" I asked Karen when she reentered the room.

"No problem. She didn't ask for any particulars, so I didn't offer any."

We left the room and returned to the porch where Sgt. Kennett was talking to another uniformed policeman. He broke away from the conversation and joined us.

"Doc, how long do you think this guy's been dead?" Kennett asked.

I deferred to my partner. "Karen, what do you think?"

"At least a couple of days. He's beginning to bloat and turn green. The room isn't excessively warm."

"That works for me," Kennett replied. "The roommate said he hadn't seen Robert since Monday night. It's been two days. Thanks."

"Hey, Sarge." I called to Kennett as he turned away. "Did the roommate mention anything about the decedent doing this before?"

"No. He's the one who discovered the body and was genuinely surprised by all the porno magazines and the mirror.

He knew Robert liked to look at the centerfolds, but that was about all."

"Thanks, Sergeant. We'll see you later."

As Karen and I stepped off the porch, we noticed that a crowd had begun to gather. We had to navigate our way around a small boy sitting on a tricycle in the middle of the front walk. I wondered what the little boy would hear about the death that had occurred inside and hoped some tact would be used if someone tried to explain autoerotic death to him. Most adults, let alone a young child, wouldn't understand this type of case. Lost in my own thoughts, I stepped off the curb into the same puddle of water that had previously soaked my trouser leg. This time I drenched the other leg. I only sighed and climbed into the car.

A few blocks away, Karen began to vent.

"Why didn't Gus call me himself about this case? I'm on duty today and he knows it. Or did he just assume that I wouldn't be interested?"

"Karen, relax. He wanted to share the case with both of us. He told me to be sure and ask you to come along."

"Yeah . . . like a little puppy dog. You'd better tell him to call me first when I'm on duty. I'm supposed to be working on these cases also. I don't think he likes me, and I know he doesn't respect me."

"Why do you say that? He likes you . . . it's just. . . ."

"Just what?"

I hesitated because I really didn't want to discuss her personality defects right now. "You can be a little aggressive at times. I think that turns him off."

"Turns him off! What am I supposed to do, turn him on?"

"I didn't mean that."

"Well, what did you mean?"

"Just what I said. You tend to be too aggressive. I don't think you need to be."

"But I'm a woman and I need to act a certain way in order to gain respect for the position I hold."

"You can save the speech, Karen. I've heard it before. All I'm saying is that you'll probably get better results if you treat these guys like equals. The respect will naturally follow."

"I think you're defending him just because you're friends."

"Gus knows you're a professional, but you could be right. Maybe I am defending him. We've been good friends for many years."

Karen frowned, slumped back in her seat, and said nothing during the rest of the trip back to the office.

7

The morning of the Thomas funeral was windy and uncomfortably cool. I tried to avoid funerals whenever I could. I didn't need to be a part of putting the same person in the ground I had worked on in the morgue. Most of the social aspects of the funeral process seemed to me to be grossly extravagant and even superfluous, so I usually refused to attend the visitations and the services at the church. This one however, I couldn't avoid.

I tightened my overcoat collar because of the chill. Standing close enough to the proceedings to see the minister and the grim-faced mourners gathered around the grave site, I was surprised that so few people were attending this outdoor service. The temperature probably kept most people away.

The minister stood on a slightly elevated piece of ground

directly in front of the family. He was close to finishing his comments when I arrived. I recognized a number of the physicians who were associates of Dr. Thomas. Mary was sitting regally stiff with her eyes directed forward. She appeared strong with a stern visage. I guessed she was intent on not showing much emotion. Seated to her left was her son and to the right, a woman I didn't know, probably the sister from New York I had never met.

The minister finished speaking and the grim members of the crowd waited for Mary to stand before they hustled back to the warmth of their automobiles. I walked towards Mary's limousine, hoping I could speak to her before she entered her car. For some reason I felt the urge to let her know I was present.

I arrived at her car as the funeral director was opening the door.

"Mark, thanks for coming," she sighed as she grabbed my arm firmly above the elbow. Behind her was the woman I had seen seated next to her.

"Dr. Jamison, this is Grace, my sister."

I nodded my greeting while shaking Grace's hand. Grace resembled Mary, but a few years younger.

"Mary, I don't want to hold you up, but I wanted to come and pay my respects."

John Jr. was standing next to Grace. He gave me a disapproving look so I decided to cut my conversation short.

Junior urged his mother and aunt into the back seat of the limo and closed the door. He quickly stepped around to the other side of the car and disappeared from view. The funeral director hastily slid behind the wheel and started the engine.

"Call me tomorrow," Mary mouthed as the limo pulled away.

I called as Mary had requested and within a few days I was standing on her doorstep for the second time. The neighborhood and the house didn't intimidate me as much as they had during my first visit.

Mary opened the door herself. She was dressed in a stylish two-piece beige suit.

"Thank you for coming, Mark. I hope this wasn't a problem."

"Not at all. I'm glad you called."

"Please come into the library. Dinner will be ready shortly."

She led me into the same room as last time, and almost by habit I chose the same chair as I had before. The difference this time was that Mary slid her chair closer to mine, facing me. I was impressed by her composure and if she was grieving, she was doing an excellent job of masking her true feelings. I looked into her eyes and discovered her youthful vitality from 20 years ago had evolved into a seasoned beauty and grace that I found to be incredibly attractive.

"Would you like anything to drink?"

"No, I'm fine for now." Actually I would have liked something to drink, but I wanted to be fully alert and professional in this situation.

"Just let me know when you're ready. Mark, tell me again how you think John died."

I quickly forgot about alcohol and became all business. "John had a diseased heart. I believe he died of an arrhythmia, an abnormal heartbeat."

"Mark, I know what an arrhythmia is. I am a doctor's wife

and I've heard more than I ever wanted to know about medicine, especially orthopedic surgery. I am familiar with many medical terms."

"I'm sorry, I didn't mean to be patronizing. His coronary arteries were in bad shape and there was evidence of at least two old heart attacks."

"I guess that explains the chest pain."

"Chest pain?"

"Yes, he complained of it on and off for more than two years. We discussed his symptoms and he tried to convince me it was just indigestion. Later I began to suspect his heart was involved, but when I tried to broach the subject, he didn't want to talk about it. He wouldn't have gone to a doctor anyway. He's kind of hardheaded. I mean was."

Many people find it difficult to speak about a recent loss, but Mary was dealing with the issue with resolve and dignity. I found her strength to be very inspiring.

"Mary, you didn't appear shocked when I first came by to tell you about John's death."

"Mark, I don't know how to explain it, but I wasn't surprised at all. John wasn't in very good shape. He was overweight, didn't get any exercise, and smoked those horrible cigars. I tried to persuade him to go in for a physical, give up smoking, and cut back on the fat and cholesterol, but he seemed to think he was immune to getting sick. Besides, I know the kind of work you do and when you appeared in my foyer, I knew the news couldn't be good. It was only a matter of time before John's deplorable living habits would catch up with him."

After her explanation, I had little more to say. Mary, reticent as well, continued to watch me until the tension seemed almost palpable. Thankfully the library doors opened and the housekeeper announced dinner.

"Excuse me, Mrs. Thomas. Dinner is ready to be served."

"Thank you, Luisa," Mary responded. She stood up and motioned for me to follow. The dining room was no less exquisite than the parts of the house I had already seen. The furniture was a rich, red cherry. Deeply grained wood wainscoting covered the lower half of the walls up to a subtle linen wallpaper. Green velvet drapes added warmth to the overall atmosphere. The table seated at least 10; however, only two places were set at one end. Mary took the chair at the head of the table and she told me to sit in the chair to her right. I felt as though I were on a date at a five-star restaurant.

"Please have a seat. Luisa, you may begin serving."

Luisa stepped into the kitchen and reappeared momentarily with our salad course. I sat there thinking that this million-dollar house with its carefully trained servants and manicured landscaping was definitely out of my league. On the other hand, Mary seemed perfectly at ease and comfortable in her surroundings. We had grown so far apart in the last two decades.

The dinner was impressive. Sautéed mushrooms and a delicately broiled red snapper constituted the main course, followed by a homemade lemon tart for dessert. Luisa continually refilled our glasses with an aged French wine, the final contribution to a perfect evening. The conversation never lagged and while there was no mention of her husband's death during the dinner, Mary did talk about her son.

"John Jr. has had a difficult time these last few years. He hasn't done well in school. We sent him to St. George's the last two years of high school and then he went on to Princeton.

He performed poorly during his first semester, so he dropped out and returned home. He's still trying to find himself."

"Did he flunk out?"

"Why . . . yes." Mary seemed hesitant to answer, as if her reply was an embarrassment for the family. How silly, I thought. His father's dead and she's worried about what I'll think about her son flunking out of college.

"What is he doing now?"

"Not much."

"Does he have a job?"

"Not really."

Again, Mary's reluctant and very succinct answers surprised me. I wondered why she cared at all about my opinion of her son. Just as I was searching for a different topic of conversation, she suggested we go back into the library to talk. I wasn't sure what she wanted to talk about since we'd covered almost every appropriate subject I could possibly dredge up. We reclaimed our same places before Mary spoke.

"Mark, what does it mean that John died a natural death?"

"I'm not sure what you're getting at."

"For insurance purposes," she replied without hesitation.

"Oh . . . John's life insurance policy will be paid off as soon as the claim is processed. I can help with that if you like. Sometimes I can speed up the procedure by speaking directly to the company."

"Mark, that's not exactly what I meant."

"What did you mean?"

"I mean, how much will I receive?" she whispered.

"That depends on the amount of the policy."

"It was a million dollars."

The amount didn't surprise me. I had expected it to be considerable since John was a successful and highly regarded physician.

I answered, "You'll receive that amount. The insurance company pays face value for a natural death."

Mary's reaction was not what I expected. Her anxious concern was replaced, not by a look of secure well-being, but rather by a frightened bewilderment. I couldn't believe that the thought of a million dollar payment made her feel afraid.

"What's wrong?" I asked solicitously.

"Oh, Mark, I don't even know where to begin."

"What do you mean, Mary? Tell me what's wrong."

"I hate to burden you with my problems, Mark."

"Go ahead, I think I can handle it."

"You may not believe me, but we weren't doing too well financially. John lost a lot of money on a few poorly considered business deals. The last few months have been difficult, and I know that it will be impossible for me to take care of John Jr. and myself and this house on only a million dollars."

I tried not to appear completely dumbfounded, but the degree of opulence surrounding me made Mary's explanation sound ridiculous. John must have made more than a half a million dollars a year in his practice. How serious could his debts have been? I had heard stories like this before. Wealthy physicians, wanting more, never satisfied, falling into speculative deals. Physicians seemed to be easy prey for the wheeler-dealers because they rarely had the time or the inclination to understand what to do with their money. As a rule, they were generally very poor businessmen.

"Mary, surely your financial advisors will have a strategy

in place for you to maintain your current lifestyle and to pay off your husband's debts."

"Do you remember George Brower?"

"I don't know that I do. Was he a friend of your husband's?"

"Yes. Well, he once was. He's the man who many people think bilked thousands of dollars out of several local physicians a few years back. I'm sure you must have read about the situation in the paper."

"Was John one of the physicians he swindled?"

"Yes, unfortunately he was. John wouldn't tell me how much he lost, but I know it may have been more than a few million."

"I'm astonished, Mary. John had a very successful practice. Surely recouping his losses was just a matter of time?"

"That might have been true, but there's more. When he lost that money, he felt so stupid and so ashamed that he impulsively tried to make it all back that much faster. He invested heavily in another risky project with Mr. Brower. Do you know the Franklin Building?"

"Sure, I read about it. It was a disaster. Springfield wasn't quite ready for an office complex of that magnitude. I believe it's just now starting to fill up with some tenants. Many investors were forced into bankruptcy for their involvement. Was John involved as well?"

"He certainly was. John and I were forced to live with the consequences of his poor judgment. He was a wonderful father, doctor, and husband, but a very poor financial manager."

"How serious are your debts at this point?" I felt free to ask this personal question since Mary had raised the issue.

"The house is completely mortgaged and John borrowed against his life insurance."

I suddenly realized what was coming. I recalled a similar scenario from just last year. A young man had shot himself and lived long enough to get to the ER. The doctors tried unsuccessfully to save his life, but the bill for their efforts was $6,500. The father's medical insurance wouldn't cover the bill because it was a suicide, and the life insurance policy was worth only $5,000. The only way the father could pay for both the hospital bill and the burial expenses was a ruling of accidental death. An accident pays double indemnity. The father asked me if I would consider signing out his son's death as an accident. Of course I couldn't honor his request; to do so would have been not only unethical and unprofessional, but criminal as well.

"What are you asking me to do, Mary?"

"I hate to ask the question, Mark, but are you sure John's death wasn't an accident?"

"Mary, the evidence clearly shows your husband's death was not an accident. He was dead or dying from his heart disease when his car hit the bridge. There's no way I could rule this anything other than a natural death."

"Oh Mark, I would never ask you to do anything illegal. Please just forget that I even made the suggestion. Although I'm terrified at the thought of having to sell my home, and I have no idea where I'll come up with the money to cover John's debts, I would never want to receive more money from the insurance than I am entitled to."

Mary buried her face between her hands, and instinctively I rose to comfort her. I began to feel tremendous guilt that I was the cause of more pain after all that she had just been through.

Crying softly, she met my advance and nestled her head against my hip. I stroked her hair. The subtle fragrance of her perfume and her momentary weakness were intoxicating. Romantic thoughts started to muddle my thinking before I prevented myself from going too far. This woman had just been left bankrupt after losing her husband, and I was thinking like a dirty old man. Nevertheless, I didn't push her away. I just held on and appreciated the moment for all it was worth. Mary raised a very tear-stained, sad visage to meet mine, and I felt the invitation behind her eyes. I knew it was time for me to go before I made a complete fool out of myself.

"I need to be going," I said as I broke away.

"Oh, please don't rush off, Mark. I don't want you to think badly of me. The future is a little scary for me right now, but I'm a strong woman and I know things will all work out. I appreciate so much your understanding and your support. I'm not usually this emotional."

"Mary, short of breaking the law, you know that I'd do anything for you."

"I know you would, Mark. Will you call me in a few days?"

"You can count on it." I quickly took my leave, anxious to clear my mind and get it back on track. The image of Mary's distressed and painful countenance kept looming up to overshadow my more rational thoughts.

8

As I was settling in the next morning to begin my morning bagel and coffee routine, Gus stuck his head in the door and asked, "Who's on call today?"

"Karen is," I answered.

"Okay, I'll go round her up."

"Anything interesting?"

"It may be. Some guy called 911 and said he found his baby dead this morning. I don't know anything more than that."

"I should pass. Get Karen to go with you, and let me know if there's anything unusual."

"Sure thing, Doc. Oh, by the way, you have two cases this morning, both pretty straightforward." Gus grinned his lopsided grin and then hustled out the door to find Karen. After a few moments I could hear the two of them conferring in the hallway.

Shirley always placed death certificates awaiting my signature on the edge of my desk so I couldn't miss them. I started to leaf through them in a desultory fashion, signing my name to the heart attack, traffic accident, and suicide victims when I stopped abruptly at the fourth one. It was Dr. Thomas's death certificate. Mary's difficult predicament immediately imposed itself on my mind and my thoughts, already considerably confused, started to spin. Willing to do almost anything to escape this distress, I placed the Thomas certificate back on the pile. I needed to lose myself in more mundane matters.

My budget hearing with the county commissioners, never a particularly joyful event, was scheduled for the afternoon. I sifted through my budget requests and the accompanying figures, just to be sure everything was in order. Budget hearings were the least favorite of my responsibilities, but nevertheless, I wanted to be sure I was prepared and that all my requests were adequately justified. Shirley discreetly entered the room, picked up the signed death certificates from my desk, and headed towards the door. She paused when she noticed not all of them had been signed.

"Excuse me, Dr. Jamison, but you didn't finish the death certificate for Dr. Thomas."

Without glancing up, I said that I wasn't finished with the case and wanted to wait for some additional information before I made a ruling. Shirley returned the incomplete certificate to my desk and left the room. I slumped down in my chair, utterly astonished at my own behavior. What in the world was I thinking? I clearly knew the cause of death and there was no reason for my apparent hesitation to sign my name to "natural death" on the certificate. Appalled at my own ambivalence, I grabbed the budget papers and again attempted to focus on the afternoon's proceedings.

Unable to concentrate, I called down to the morgue. Bill answered after the first ring.

"Doc, are you on for today?"

"Yes, I'm the cutter this morning. Dr. Lipper is out on a call. What do you have?" I already knew there were a couple of cases from my brief discussion with Gus, but I gave Bill the pleasure of letting me know what I was in for.

"You have some guy found dead in his bathtub and another guy who was homeless."

"I'll be down in a while."

"Sure thing, Doc." Bill sounded pleased. We had been a team for only a short time but we worked well together. He knew I was fast and he liked to have his autopsy room cleaned up by noon if possible. After that he didn't have much to do except for the odd jobs Gus asked him to perform.

Thoughts of Mary still weighed on my mind. Once my soulmate, Mary had left me because she didn't want to wait all those years for me to finish medical school and then a residency. The irony of it was that she ended up with a doctor anyway. Of course the one she chose made millions more than I ever would or could, undoubtedly proving her theory that we had grown too far apart to ever make a go of things. Seeing her again though, only reinforced my memories of an incredibly close, meaningful relationship that had been too casually tossed aside.

I had to quit thinking of her. Maybe my work would allow me to erase her from my mind, at least for awhile. I headed downstairs to do the morning's cases.

I found Bill in the coffee room, singing along to some country music and drinking a cup of coffee. He acted embarrassed when he saw me.

"I'm sorry, Doc. I didn't think you'd be here so soon. I'm not quite ready with the bodies."

"No problem, Bill. I just decided to come down a little early. Go ahead and get the first one out while I change my clothes."

"Do you have a preference?" he asked.

"Not unless one of them is decomposed, in which case I'd like to do that one last."

"Nah, they're both fresh, although the homeless guy might smell a little."

"Let's do him last then." The smell of an unwashed body was particularly repugnant to me, far more than the odor of decomposition.

The first case was the man who had been discovered dead in his bathtub. These cases could be problematic due to the difficulty of distinguishing between a sudden death occurring in the bathtub and a drowning caused by heart attack or seizure. Luckily this case was an easy one. Bill had discovered the cause of death as soon as he removed the top of the man's skull.

"Look at this, Doc," Bill exclaimed.

A tremendous amount of blood was covering the top of the decedent's brain.

"He must have ruptured an aneurysm," Bill immediately concluded. He had assisted autopsies for only six months but he was a quick study. Attending night school because he wanted to be a doctor, he rarely forgot what he'd been taught.

"So I guess one of the blood vessel's walls must have gotten weak over time and ballooned out before it finally ruptured. He probably died very quickly, don't you think, Doc?"

"Absolutely right, Bill."

"But did he drown?"

"No. It wouldn't have mattered if he were taking a bath or shoveling snow. He would have died suddenly regardless of where he was or what he had been doing."

I took about 10 minutes to wash the blood off the bottom of the brain in order to isolate the site of the rupture. I found the torn balloon and asked Bill to take a photograph of it for me while I dictated the results of the autopsy. Bill, always eager when I gave him more responsibilities, jumped at the opportunity to play photographer as well as morgue assistant.

After the dictation, I drank a cup of coffee and waited for Bill to ready the next body.

Within 15 minutes, Bill had the homeless man on the table, ready for examination. This entire case took less than 45 minutes. With no visible signs of injury or disease, I surmised that the man was probably a chronic alcoholic. We retrieved blood and urine for a drug screen. I knew that chronic alcoholics can die suddenly with little or no alcohol in their system, so I didn't expect the drug screen to necessarily be positive for drugs or alcohol.

I thanked Bill for his assistance, changed my clothes, and was leaving the autopsy suite when I met Gus and Karen charging through the door. They were heatedly discussing something about the scene they had just visited. I could only pick up a little of the conversation as the two of them marched up to me.

"I don't think we know that for sure," Gus was saying.

"Of course we do. The guy wrapped the baby up. You heard him," Karen countered.

"Let's wait and see what the autopsy shows, okay?" Gus replied, anxious to end the discussion.

Karen stopped in front of me, obviously exasperated. She rarely seemed to find that middle ground of mellow, laid-back satisfaction that I so clearly enjoyed.

"Problem?" I asked.

"No problem. Gus and I talked to the baby's father at the scene. He told us the baby was wrapped tightly in the blanket and was discovered face down on the mattress. He wasn't breathing. It sounded to me like he wrapped the child up to keep it quiet. Gus doesn't agree. At least he's not willing to commit to that yet. We'll just have to wait until the autopsy."

"The man never directly said that he wrapped the baby up. And he certainly didn't admit to wrapping the baby in a blanket to keep it quiet. It's entirely possibly that the baby became tangled in the blanket on its own," Gus interjected.

Karen, ready for battle, wanted to say more, but I decided to end the discussion.

"Do you want to get some lunch?" I directed my question at the two combatants.

"Well . . . no, I have a bunch of work to get caught up on, and I wanted to get started writing up the case I presented at last week's conference. I also told the police at the scene that I would begin the baby's autopsy at 1:00." Karen's anger was slowly dissipating.

"Sounds good. I'll check in with you after I meet with the county commissioners."

"What's that all about?" she asked.

"Oh, nothing. Just some discussions about the budget," I answered, trying to make it sound benign.

"The budget? Do I have anything to worry about?" Karen's attention was completely focused on my response.

"Of course not. I'll let you know if there are any problems." I knew that anything discussed at the meeting was open to the public through the media. If there were problems, I'd have to tell her about them prior to her reading about it in the paper.

Gus also declined, saying he had consumed a gargantuan breakfast that was still giving him trouble.

We parted company, agreeing to talk again later. I passed the lunch hour scanning the budget again and briefly falling asleep in front of my computer. I belonged to a list server with the academy where members could write about anything that came to mind. Occasionally there were interesting cases for discussion or some member would present a problem needing an enlightened solution. Sometimes it was a very intellectual forum, but today I dozed off. I almost missed my budget meeting.

9

The commissioners' chambers were in the 60-year-old courthouse that was soon to be replaced by a new edifice being built one block north. This would probably be the last time I appeared in this old building for business. Built with federal money at a time when gray limestone was in vogue, the building was designed around a central rotunda that gave the impression of a much more expansive structure. There were two floors above the ground before the domed, colorful ceiling capped off the open space. After climbing the marble staircase to the commission's chambers, I relaxed on the wooden bench outside the entrance and instinctively pulled a new western from my coat pocket. I had been reading only a few minutes before a well-dressed, middle-aged assistant appeared and asked me to follow her.

I knew where to sit since I'd been here before. The glossy conference table with two microphones was positioned directly in front of the three commissioners. The presiding commissioner, Stanley Garland, smiled as I took my seat. We had known each other ever since he had worked as a volunteer fireman for the county, and we'd met at the site of a traffic accident in which the driver of the car had been burned beyond recognition. I could still remember the look on his face after seeing the extensively charred remains. I thought he was going to be physically sick, but he'd managed to somehow repress his nausea. Of the three commissioners, Stan was definitely my biggest supporter.

"Welcome, Dr. Jamison. Thanks for coming. This shouldn't take too long. We wanted to talk to you about your proposed budget. Before we begin, I would like to go on record as saying that our county has always been fortunate to have someone of your caliber as medical examiner." Always the politician, it was obvious he wanted everyone in the room, including the reporters, to know that he had no problems with my budget.

"Now then. We have just a few questions. First of all, I want to remind the commissioners that the estimates you've made in the past concerning numbers of cases you anticipate for the next year have never been very far off. The problem we have, or I should say the county has, is a projected shortfall in revenue. According to our charter, the county is not allowed to operate in the red. In order to prevent any problems, we have to look at every department and see where the county might be able to save some money."

After reciting his very predictable piece, Stan asked if either of the other two commissioners had anything to say before turning the floor over to the county auditor, Mr. Tamper. There was no response, so the auditor was given the floor.

"Good afternoon, Dr. Jamison." The auditor was a portly man in his fifties who sported a flattop haircut and always wore a suit that was one size too small. He reminded me of an old drill sergeant whose muscles had turned to fat and commanded respect only through his rank and the use of force. "I've been looking at your budget and see that your autopsy numbers were about the same last year as they were the year before. Yet last year you requested funds to hire a part-time pathologist, funds that the commission generously granted. Would you like to discuss the possibility of eliminating this part-time position since you predict that your number of autopsies will remain stable? This would save the county a considerable amount of money."

Although I'd anticipated this issue would come up, I hadn't expected it to be addressed so early in the questioning. We were talking about a particular person, not just a position. I could hear the reporters behind me scribbling on their notepads. The news of the possible elimination of Karen's job would be too late for today's newspaper, but it was sure to be on the six o'clock newscast and on the front page tomorrow morning.

"With all due respect, eliminating the position is not an option. I thought I made a good case for this position before, and the reasons for my request remain the same. Even though the autopsy numbers are stable, our overall caseload is up. The autopsy numbers also don't reflect that the office is doing more traumatic deaths and children. These types of cases take much more time to investigate than other types. I won't let this office regress to its previous deplorable state. Asking a medical examiner to work entirely on his own, taking call 24 hours a day, seven days a week, and still expecting him to treat each case professionally and personally with no help whatsoever is ludicrous. It doesn't take a rocket scientist to realize that overwork causes mistakes and eventual burnout. You'll end up replacing medical examiners faster than you replace mayors in this town. Forensic pathology is a legitimate, necessary medical specialty and as such, it deserves the county's respect and due consideration."

My speech was issued with more vehemence than I usually displayed at such hearings. I guess I didn't feel like ingratiating myself to this body. I never liked appearing before the commissioners, probably because they seemed too much like politicians and too little like public servants. The auditor's irritating attitude rubbed me the wrong way and I was offended. But I knew I had to remain civil even if it was painful to do so.

Stan defused the situation. "Do we have anything else for Dr. Jamison?"

One of the other commissioners, Gladys Marberry, spoke. "I believe the auditor raises a good point. I would like to see the need for an assistant to Dr. Jamison discussed more thoroughly in the near future." She seemed to making the statement solely for her constituency.

"I agree with you, Gladys," Stan said. "We'll review the matter again in a few weeks. Is everyone in agreement?" Stan seemed to be doing his best to end the discussion and move on to the next department. I wasn't quite sure who he wanted to save today. Maybe he didn't want me to lose control, or maybe he didn't want the auditor to look like a hardass in a public meeting.

I glanced over to Stan and nodded my thanks. He barely

moved his head in recognition. As I scooted my chair back, Stan was already calling Greene County Sheriff Tim Copeland to present his department's budget.

My drive back to the office was not a pleasant one. I began thinking about all of the possible cuts I could make, if the commission forced me to do so, but I also knew that I would not allow the department to take a step backwards. I wouldn't do the job again without an assistant. If the commissioners couldn't find a way to keep Karen on board, I'd have to decide how important the job was to me. I certainly didn't relish finding another position at this time in my career.

I arrived at the office without resolving in my own mind how I would handle the situation. Noticing a few extra cars in the parking lot, I assumed they belonged to law enforcement that were still here for the autopsy of the baby that Karen and Gus had argued about earlier. I decided to bypass the morgue and go straight to my office. I hoped Gus and Karen had resolved their disagreement over the case, but I knew they'd find me if there were still problems.

I was looking at some slides under the microscope when both Gus and Karen exploded into my office after a brief knock at the door.

"Hi, come on in and have a seat." Any hopes I'd had for them reaching a consensus were dashed when I saw their faces. I leisurely sat back, feeling like a parent having to negotiate a squabble between warring siblings.

Karen immediately presented her case.

"I just finished the autopsy on the five-week-old boy that was discovered dead by his father this morning. Gus and I have a difference of opinion on both the cause and manner of death.

I believe the cause should be suffocation due to chest compression and the manner homicide."

"I didn't say I disagreed with you," Gus responded with an uncharacteristic firmness I hadn't heard in a while. He usually reserved this manner of speaking for times in which he was very frustrated or very mad. This time he was both.

"You most certainly did!" Karen countered.

"Hold on." I stopped them before tempers escalated to a point where irrationality would rule. "Tell me what's going on. I need some background information so I can have some feeling for the issues. Karen, tell me what you know."

Karen attempted to compose herself. She began speaking urgently as if she expected to be interrupted at any moment.

"The father said he found his baby face down, wrapped up in a blanket about three hours after he fed him and put him to bed. I think he wrapped the baby up so tightly that he couldn't breathe and placed him face down. Because of that, the child couldn't move his head, and he suffocated. If he did that, it's a homicide. The autopsy proved no other cause of death besides suffocation. I'm ready to rule the death a homicide due to suffocation."

Gus was chomping at the bit. He started to interrupt Karen while she was talking, but held his tongue.

"Gus, tell me what you think went on here."

Gus hesitated for a moment before he began. Because of his police training, I knew he didn't particularly enjoy disagreeing with a superior. Old habits die hard. He picked his words very carefully.

"I'd like to start from the beginning. We went to the scene of a dead baby. The father said he discovered the baby dead at about 6:30 A.M. when the alarm went off. He had to get the baby up and feed him before his wife returned from work. She works the graveyard shift at the hospital as a LPN. The father said he found the baby with the blanket wrapped around him and covering his head. He lifted the baby and tried to get the blanket off. It was difficult to remove. Dr. Lipper asked him if the blanket was wrapped around the baby and he said he thought so but couldn't remember."

"You forgot to mention he admitted placing the baby face down after he wrapped him up and put him to bed," Karen interrupted and continued. "And that's why I think this is a homicide. That baby would still be alive today if he hadn't wrapped it up to keep it from crying."

"He never said he wrapped the baby up!" Gus's voice was louder now. "He said he placed the child face down and put the blanket around him. The only time he said the baby was wrapped was when you asked him if it looked like the blanket was wrapped around him and he said he thought so, but couldn't remember. You can't rule this a homicide because of what you 'think' the man did!"

Karen's voice rose to match Gus's. "You didn't mention the bruise on the baby's arm or the blanching on the baby's face."

"That bruise was discovered later at the autopsy. That's your area of expertise and I'll leave it to you to explain what you think." Gus was struggling to regain his composure and let Karen discuss those issues she knew best.

"Karen, what about the bruising and the blanching?" I asked.

"There was a bruise on the baby's right arm. Someone either hit the baby or grabbed him tightly. He couldn't get a bruise like that from falling because he couldn't walk. The blanching on the nose, actually on the side of the face, shows the baby was placed face down after he was wrapped."

"Or maybe he died on his face naturally, and the face became pale because he was in that position when he died. That doesn't prove he died of suffocation."

Karen didn't have time to respond to Gus's last salvo because I cut off the discussion.

"Thanks, I think I get the picture." This was one of those rare occasions when I was going to have to play the role of superior officer, a role I truly despised, but it was obvious that I had to intervene. There was no way these two headstrong individuals were going to agree on anything about this case.

"Gus, I want either you or the police to interrogate the father again. I don't care if you accuse him of murder or not. Shake him up a little and see if his story remains the same. Listen carefully to see if he mentions wrapping the baby in the blanket."

Gus nodded in agreement.

"Karen, we should wait until all the information is in to make a ruling. I agree that bruising of a baby who can't walk yet is suspicious and that's why I want the father interrogated more. Since this is a potential homicide, I want to wait until the tox results and the microscopic examinations are complete before we put it all together. When we have all the results, including completed investigations, then you can make a final ruling. One thing I don't want to do is jump to homicide when all the facts aren't in. Can you agree to that?"

Karen couldn't argue with my common-sense approach. She was a well-trained pathologist, just young and a bit impulsive. Her look betrayed hurt and embarrassment, but she was smart enough to keep her mouth shut at this point and to follow my lead. She mutely left the office, followed resolutely by Gus.

One thing I hated was confrontation. It was easier when only Gus, Bill, Shirley, and I were in the office. I don't remember the four of us ever having such a disagreement. That's because we all worked together as a team. Everyone knew I was the boss but we considered ourselves to be colleagues with a common goal of finding the answers to each case as a team. I doubted that Karen and Gus ever felt like they were part of the same team.

I eased back in my chair and closed my eyes. I was thankful for the peace and quiet, even though it seemed like only a split second before the phone rang.

"Dr. Jamison, Mrs. Thomas is on the line. She said it's not an emergency, but she would like to speak to you. Will you take the call?" said Shirley, coolly professional.

"Absolutely." This would definitely brighten my day.

"Mark, this is Mary. I hope I'm not bothering you."

"No, not at all. What can I do for you?"

"I'm not quite sure how to ask this, so I'm just going to come right to the point. Would you have dinner with me tonight? I've been feeling lonely since our last meeting, and I would like to have some company, but I don't want you to feel obligated to say yes."

My response took less than a nanosecond. "Of course. Will we be eating at your house again? I thoroughly enjoyed our meal together there."

"No, not at the house. I already had a place picked out in

hopes you would say yes. The Top of the Dome, downtown, has a highly regarded restaurant, or at least so I've been told. Does that sound appealing? We could go somewhere else if you'd like."

"That sounds perfect. May I pick you up?"

"No, let's meet there about seven. And Mark, I hope you don't think me too forward for asking you to dinner. I don't want you to think badly of me."

"Don't worry about it. I look forward to seeing you."

I had to admit I was surprised by the invitation. A woman like Mary must have had many friends who could help fill up her lonely hours. I hardly thought of myself as a scintillating dinner partner. Nevertheless, I wanted to believe that she truly enjoyed my company. Perhaps the fact that I was an old friend and in essence, an outsider in terms of her social group, might make me a more comfortable companion, especially in terms of her current financial situation.

I relegated the problems with the budget and the disagreement between Gus and Karen to the back of my mind. It was surprisingly easy to do so. Even though Mary had discounted the invitation as a date, I felt as if dinner was one. The thought of "dating" again made me feel a bit queasy, but somehow I thought I could get used to the idea, especially with a woman as attractive and beguiling as Mary. Any other time I would have chastised myself for doing what I was doing, seeing a recently widowed woman before she had time to grieve, but I rationalized that this was a unique situation and I'd be foolish to pass up such an incredible opportunity.

Before I rose from my chair, I noticed the death certificate of Dr. Thomas still resting on the corner of the desk. Without giving it another thought, I decided to go home to shower and change clothes.

Grabbing my jacket, I told Shirley I was done for the day and left the building. I usually stopped by the morgue at the end of the day to check on any new arrivals, but today I just didn't want to bother.

The drive home was filled with the shameless anticipation of seeing Mary. I barely noticed the dogs other than to open the back door and let them out. I poured myself a glass of wine, went through the mail and paper, and then took a leisurely shower. What to wear momentarily bewildered me, but my newest tweed sport coat looked almost up-to-date, and I selected a light blue chambray shirt because Shirley always complimented me when I wore that color. I couldn't remember when I had last given any thought at all to what I was wearing. I felt like a giddy adolescent getting ready for his first date.

When 6:20 rolled around I was ready to go. I drove to the hotel and used valet parking, something I rarely did. I was 20 minutes early so I went into the bar and ordered a bourbon and water. The bartender and I struck up a conversation about the St. Louis Cardinals, and after talking on and off for a half an hour and consuming two drinks, Mary arrived.

10

She looked absolutely stunning in a black, knee-length dress with spaghetti straps that flowed easily over the curves of her body. Maybe she looked better because of the drinks I'd bolted down while waiting, but whatever the reason, I was elated to be in her company.

"I'm sorry I'm late," she whispered as she kissed me on the cheek. She smelled as if she had just stepped out of the shower. Her fragrance instantly brought back memories of when we'd lived together. I was surprised that her smell would jar such an ancient recollection.

Mary must have guessed something was on my mind because she asked if anything was wrong.

"Not at all. Are you ready to eat, or would you like a drink first?"

"Let's go ahead and grab a table; there's always time for drinks during and after dinner."

She casually looped her arm thorough mine as we signaled the maitre d' that we were ready to be seated. He smiled at Mary as if they were old friends. I mentioned that we had reservations, although he didn't even check the schedule before leading us to a secluded table in the corner. Mary had implied over the phone that she had never been to this restaurant before; however, her actions seemed to indicate otherwise. But then Mary was a sophisticated woman and I knew that she probably donned the appropriate demeanor for each and every social situation in which she found herself. It was hard to imagine her ever feeling uncomfortable or ill at ease anywhere.

After we were seated, the waiter asked for our drink orders. Mary took charge and ordered some wine, whose name I'd never heard of. She was a welcome change from other women I'd known who couldn't make the simplest decision without considerable effort.

"I hope you don't mind me picking the wine. I know it isn't cold duck," she joked, reminding me of the many cheap bottles of wine we'd consumed long ago.

"You haven't forgotten," I said with surprise.

"How could I? You were the love of my life then."

I momentarily thought of our time together and remembered how hopelessly in love I'd been. I wondered if it was happening to me again.

"You haven't forgotten the good times, have you?" she asked.

I looked straight into those amazing eyes and said, "Of course not. We had something special."

"I know we did, and I'm the one who let it slip away," Mary responded with a downward glance.

"Mary, that was a long time ago and we were young. I don't think either one of us was very mature back then."

"I guess not," she agreed.

"Let's talk about something else. We shouldn't dwell on old memories."

"You're right," she brightened.

"Tell me about yourself. I mean, before John's death," I said.

Mary proceeded to give me her life's story after we had split up. She told me she had met John about a year after she graduated from college. He was just beginning his residency at the time and she found him to be a welcome relief from other college guys who were only looking for a quick roll in the hay, not a long-term commitment. She hadn't dated anyone seriously since our breakup, and John turned up to fill the void.

"We had a really solid relationship at the beginning. I tried to be the perfect doctor's wife and John was incredibly caring and unselfish. But after John Jr. was born, I threw myself into mothering, and John became focused on his career. I'm not sure what happened in all those years. I just know that we lost the intimacy and the part of us that was close. We gradually drifted apart, until the last few years when we were just going through the motions of a marriage. I had everything money could buy, but romantically our marriage left a lot to be desired. John must have felt the same way."

"I'm surprised you didn't do more with your degree. You were so wrapped up in your sociology; I was sure you'd end up doing something with abused children. What happened?"

"I honestly don't know, Mark. John was happiest with me not working, and after the years went by, I ended up on a different path. It always seemed too difficult to try to change it."

There was definitely regret in her voice. I don't believe she was looking for sympathy, only being sincere.

"Mary, tell me about your son. You haven't talked about him."

After a moment of hesitation, she said, "John Jr. is going through a tough time. He's an amazingly bright kid, just like his dad, but he's never really found himself. I keep hoping at some point he'll wake up and get focused, but it hasn't happened yet. I sometimes think I centered too much of my attention on him. To others I know he appears overindulged and spoiled, but I can still see the good in him. I just wish I knew how to help him."

"I'm sure he'll be fine, Mary. You obviously showered him with lots of love, and that will help him through the tough times."

She changed the subject quickly. "I want to hear about you. I've talked enough about my family and me. Have you been happy?"

"I guess so. Or I should say I thought I was until my divorce. But then I thought my wife was happy also, an obvious illusion on my part. She wanted 'more out of life than I had given her' to use her exact words. One day she just packed her things and moved out, leaving me with my memories and the two dogs. I think she was sick of me putting my job before her, and she was right. She never received my undivided attention. I guess I deserved what she did to me. I've regretted my actions ever since."

"I'm so sorry about the way things turned out for you, Mark." She reached across the table, sought out my nearest hand, and gently placed hers on the back of mine. "I'd always hoped you'd find true happiness. You've certainly made a success of your career. So many people in the community look up to you. I've followed your career ever since you became the medical examiner. You don't know how many times I've wanted to call you."

Music began to play in the background and Mary sighed. "Music is something I really miss. John didn't care much for music, unless it was at the movies. I missed it for so many years. Now that he's gone, I play my favorite old songs all the time. I wanted so much to enjoy it with him, but that wasn't possible. He never seemed to be able to relax enough to enjoy much of anything with me. After a while, I stopped trying."

"I have some good oldies at home that I'd love to share with you sometime."

"I would like that."

The conversation never faltered throughout the evening. There weren't any of those awkward periods when the silence is palpable. I felt nervous and at the same time guilty for feeling so good about being with Mary. After all, I was in the company of a recent widow who would probably have preferred to mourn in private. But I didn't care. I was doing exactly what I wanted to do and I didn't feel responsible for myself or anyone else.

Regretfully I realized that the restaurant was emptying, and it was time to end the evening.

"Mary, I've enjoyed our dinner and all the conversation. I can't tell you how much this evening means to me. Even though I know it's only temporary, I feel more alive than I've felt in a long time. I appreciate your company so much."

Mary smiled warmly and touched my hand again. "I feel the same way." The look in her eyes almost caused me to melt.

"I think we should be going. We've tied up this table long enough."

"You're right," she agreed as she glanced around at the empty tables. I wanted to believe she had enjoyed the evening as much as I had.

I rose from my chair, immediately felt light-headed, and quickly sat back down.

"I think I've had a little too much to drink."

"Mark, I've consumed much less than you. Let me drive you home. You can pick up your car later. I'd love the opportunity to take care of you for a little while. You've done so much recently to help me."

It was difficult to argue with a woman who was so decisive and clearly in control of the situation. I decided to relax and just go with the flow.

I paid for the dinner, despite Mary's protests that she'd invited me. The valet brought her immaculate white Mercedes to the front of the hotel, and Mary quickly entered on the driver's side.

"Are you sure you're all right to drive?" I inquired.

"Mark, I'm absolutely fine. Just sit back and leave everything to me." I hadn't heard words that sounded so good in quite a long time. I eased back into the luxurious passenger seat, enveloped by the smell of Mary's perfume and the richness of imported leather. Aware that I was probably slurring my words, I concentrated on clearly enunciating every syllable as I directed Mary to my house. She parked the car in the driveway, and we strolled together to the door. I started to thank her for a memorable evening when she interrupted with, "Aren't you going to invite me in?"

Who was I to argue with fate? I knew I should be feeling total surprise that a woman like Mary enjoyed my company, but actually I was so immersed in each and every moment that I didn't stop to question how or why it had all evolved. It seemed too good to analyze it unduly.

"Mary, I'd be thrilled for you to join me in my humble abode, complete with two incredibly mangy mutts." I tried to open the door quietly, but the dogs couldn't be fooled and they were all over us in a matter of seconds. I directed Mary to the sofa while I corralled the dogs in the utility room. I hastily flung some food in their bowls to keep them quiet.

I grabbed a half-full bottle of an inexpensive White Zinfandel from the refrigerator and poured two glasses. Mary was waiting for me on my tired old sofa with an expectant twinkle playing around her eyes.

"I hope this is okay. I don't have the best taste in wine."

"Whatever you have will be fine."

"You said you like music. I have something I think you'd appreciate."

I went to the cupboard and brought out a compilation of songs on CD from the sixties and seventies. There was one I knew she would like. She used to be a big fan of the Beatles when we lived together. I started the CD and put it on the right track.

"This is something I think you'll remember."

As the magic of "Let it Be" filled the air, I knew I'd made a good choice. Mary's eyes were closed and her head was tilted back dreamily on the sofa cushion.

She spoke in a whisper. "Mark, you knew what this would do to me. You played this song on purpose. I remember exactly what we used to do when this song was playing." She eyed me suggestively, her expression both teasing and provocative.

Mary looked so inviting I couldn't resist when she motioned for me to sit next to her. She leaned back against me and I slowly began to kiss her cheek, her eyes, and finally her mouth. She responded to my efforts by reaching her hand behind my neck and pulling me closer, increasing the pressure between our lips.

Even if I'd been fully alert and sober, I know I couldn't have withstood the power of Mary at her most tempting. She was totally in control, and I was clearly happy to be led. It was a magical night, far surpassing any night that I could remember from our life before. Maturity had brought us to a new place.

I WAS JARRED AWAKE by the dogs going crazy in the utility room, scratching insistently on the door to the kitchen. I jumped out of bed, realized I was stark naked, and grabbed my shorts before I could release the dogs from their captivity. As I watched them cavorting in the backyard, I replayed the events of the night, trying to recall as much as possible. An overall feeling of intense satisfaction momentarily engulfed me, but my pounding headache brought me back to reality.

I downed a couple of aspirin with a glass of water and hastily returned to the bedroom to see if Mary was awake. The smell of her perfume still hovered in the air, but the room was empty. I heard the shower running in the bathroom and wished I were sharing that morning activity with her. But I decided to give her some private time, and waited patiently in the bedroom till she emerged, dripping, wrapped in a towel with another one wrapped around her head. She was rubbing toothpaste across her teeth with her index finger.

"I hope you don't mind. I had to get clean, and I grabbed whatever towels I could find."

"I'm happy to share," I whispered, as I came up behind her and encircled her with my arms.

"What are you doing?" she asked playfully.

"You're so irresistible." I began to loosen her towel.

"What did you have in mind?"

I whispered into her ear. "How about breakfast in bed?"

Grabbing a nearby bottle of mouthwash, she made me take a swig before she'd respond to my kisses. Then I grabbed the towel from her body and began exploring all the newly washed surfaces. Her smell was like a drug, overwhelming and so powerful, I wanted to inhale her entire body. Soon we were back in bed after a few brief stops against the wall, the dresser, and the armchair. But this time it was even better than the night before, without our senses being blunted by the effects of alcohol.

We spent the next hour and a half making love before we both determined that it was time for Mary to go home and me to go to work. After dressing hastily, we drove back to the restaurant so I could get my car. I was happy to see a different valet on duty than the one who had been there the night before. I didn't want the bubble to burst, so I refused to say goodbye. I waved as Mary drove off, feeling sated with all the lovemaking and eagerly hopeful that this was a new beginning.

11

I was still smiling when I arrived at work. Gus and Shirley both must have noticed my expression of joy because they intently scrutinized my expression. I avoided any possible questions by ducking into the men's room. A quick glance in the mirror told me I was exhausted. Well, I had stayed up late and engaged in more physical activity than I was normally accustomed to, but I wouldn't have traded it for anything. My feelings for Mary had resurfaced and the night's euphoria gave me a newly found hope for the future.

I took refuge in my office where I was able to eat my bagel without interruption. The Thomas death certificate once again caught my attention. Why was I still wavering about signing it out as a natural death? I already knew the reason. My decision directly affected Mary's future, a future I might well be a part of. Could I do anything now to jeopardize our being together? How could she want me if I was unwilling to make the slightest effort to help her in her time of need? All of a sudden people's lives were hanging in the balance based on one small decision.

I knew that the old Mark Jamison would never have hesitated to sign this certificate appropriately, no matter what was at stake. But I was a different man today than yesterday, and somehow I felt I'd been given a new lease on life. I'd always played by the rules, doing what was right, and look where it had gotten me. I didn't want to play it safe any more. I'd been granted one more very unexpected opportunity for happiness, and I didn't want to blow it. The decision was so obvious. I signed out the cause of death as blunt trauma to the chest and ruled it an accident. Placing the death certificate squarely on the desk so Shirley could send it off, I turned my attention to other matters.

"Good morning," I said as I stuck my head in Karen's door. She was engrossed in studying a slide under the microscope, but she still managed to reply with a terse greeting.

"Good morning to you."

"Anything going on today?"

"Not too much. There was a traffic accident over on Highway 65. A truck swiped a guardrail, overturned, and burst into flames. The driver escaped, but a passenger wasn't so lucky. The truck was carrying thousands of wieners that literally exploded all over the highway. Gus took some good photos."

"What about the passenger? Is an autopsy necessary?"

"I thought I'd better do one because the victim wasn't supposed to be in the truck. She was the driver's girlfriend, and the driver's wife isn't going to be too happy with the news."

"When are you going to do that one?" I asked.

"In about an hour. The case should be straightforward," she said, implying that I needn't bother checking up on her work. It was obvious she was still upset about my intervention in her case the day before.

"I thought you would've known about the accident. It was all over the media last night."

"I didn't watch the news. I was involved with something else." I didn't explain and Karen didn't ask.

"Let me know if you come across anything good. I can always use some good thermal injury photos." As I turned to leave the room Karen asked me if I had seen the morning paper.

"No, not yet."

"You might be interested in one of the front page articles." She didn't volunteer any other information, so I told her I'd check it out.

I went straight to Shirley and asked if she had the morning paper. She retrieved her copy from the wastebasket and handed it to me. I didn't think my meeting with the commissioners would have warranted much attention by the media, but once again I was wrong. Fortunately, my name wasn't in the headlines, but I was mentioned in the first paragraph as one of the department heads whose office was projected to be over budget. It was reported that I had been unable to propose any solutions for the eventual shortfall. Unfortunately, Karen's position was also considered newsworthy. Knowing how upset she must be, I returned to her office, only to discover she had gone down to the morgue.

She had already begun the external exam on the truck driver's dead girlfriend. No one else was in the room except for Bill and I asked him to give us a minute alone.

"Karen, I should have told you about what happened at the commissioner's meeting yesterday, but I really didn't think it was all that significant. I knew the media might latch onto it, but the budget was tabled for further discussion, so no final decision was made. I still don't think there's much to worry about."

"I wish you'd discussed it with me. You know I love this work and this town, and whatever decision the commission makes directly affects my future. I've tried to be both professional and responsible and uphold my duties in this job. Obviously the commission doesn't think my work is necessary," she said plaintively.

"Please accept my apology, Karen. You're absolutely right. I should have talked to you right after the meeting. From now on you'll be the first to know anything that comes from the commission."

Softening somewhat, she responded, "Thanks, Mark, I'd really appreciate that. It's hard to maintain my focus when I feel as though my job here may be in jeopardy." She quickly changed the subject. "This will be an excellent case for some photos. There are some perfect skin splits, thermal fractures, and a fine example of pugilistic attitude."

She was right. The woman's elbows had contracted due to the heat. And with her bent wrists and fingers closed in two fists, she appeared as if she were boxing. I momentarily wondered how many people actually knew that a pugilist was a boxer. The slides of phenomenon in my collection were old and faded, so a few new ones would be a welcome addition. I also wanted a picture of the inside of her windpipe that should show that she inhaled smoke if she were alive at the time of the fire.

"Do you know if she was alive at the time of the fire?" I asked.

"Witnesses said they heard her screaming. The firemen thought she must have caught her foot or leg in some of the wreckage and couldn't get out."

"What a horrible way to die," I said quietly.

After a few minutes Karen opened the neck area and we saw abundant soot in her trachea and larynx, indicating she was breathing during the fire. I put the camera away and thanked Karen for allowing me to hold her up by taking photos.

"No problem," she said.

"And Karen. I promise to talk to you first about anything to do with the budget or anything else that might affect your job."

"Thanks, Mark."

As I was leaving, Gus caught me in the doorway. He was carrying a box.

"What do you have, Gus?"

"Doc, I just came from the east side of the county where some bones were discovered. Several young boys were out riding their bikes near the railroad tracks, saw a culvert under a road that looked interesting, and decided to investigate. When they saw a skull they rushed home to tell their parents. The parents called it in."

"Do the police have any more information?"

"It seems that some homeless guys were living in this culvert a few months ago, but they're gone now. There's evidence of some sort of fire in the culvert because there was ash and soot everywhere. One end of the culvert appeared to have been blocked off before the fire. Let me show you the bones we found."

Gus took the box to our second morgue table and began removing six small paper bags. He handed the one marked "skull" to me. I removed a blackened skull with no upper teeth and placed it on the table. Anticipating my every need, Gus retrieved my camera from the drawer and handed it to me.

"Gus, was the mandible found?"

"No, there was nothing like the lower jaw out there. Some animal must have dragged it away," he surmised.

"That's too bad, because it might have helped to identify this person. Although with the absence of the upper teeth, I doubt if having the lower jaw would have mattered. Does anyone have an idea who it might be?"

"Law enforcement thinks it's a guy from Arkansas. Let me check the name." Gus brought out a thin notepad from his breast pocket. It was similar to ones most homicide detectives used. He flipped over a few pages and found the name.

"They think it's Bill Miller, a guy from Excelsior Springs. He lived there with his parents several weeks of the year and then he and a few other guys used to live here the rest of the year. They sometimes lived in the culvert if they couldn't find anyplace else to hang out. Since he hasn't been seen around here in quite awhile, the police are checking with the parents to find out when he was last home. The guy is supposed to be about 50 and a Vietnam vet."

I turned my attention to the skull to look for injuries. There was a large piece of the skull missing on the left side, but I thought it was caused by the fire or perhaps some animals that gnawed away a good portion. However, on closer inspection I discovered a linear groove beginning at the back part of the hole and extending for at least two inches.

"Look at this, Gus." I pointed to the groove.

"It looks like someone beat the crap out of him, or at least out of his head," Gus responded.

"Sure does, but with what?"

I rummaged around in the drawer and finally found a magnifying glass to examine the defect more closely. The outside edge of the groove was almost a quarter inch wide while the depth came to a sharp point.

"The weapon that caused this was a heavy, sharp object, something like a machete. What do you think?"

"Maybe." Gus thought for a moment and then said, "What about an ax or a hatchet? They're a little easier to find than a machete."

"You're right," I agreed. "I'm overlooking the obvious."

"Should I give the detectives a call?"

"Sure. Tell them that we'll be getting the anthropologist over here as soon as we can to narrow down the age and race."

Gus went to his office, and I grabbed the nearest phone to call upstairs.

"Shirley, would you try to locate Dr. McWilliams for me?"

"Be glad to. I've got the number right here." Shirley knew exactly who I was talking about, because she'd had a crush on him for years. Tim McWilliams was a lean, handsome professor who sported a well-trimmed beard and a full head of reddish brown hair. Over the years, Shirley had commented more than once about how attractive she found men like McWilliams with all that red hair.

I didn't have to wait very long. Tim taught a forensic bone course as well as a popular anthropology class for undergraduates at the university. He was always interested when we had a collection of bones to identify, and he planned to stop by first thing in the morning on his way to class.

I spent the rest of the afternoon organizing the remaining bones from the other five bags so McWilliams wouldn't have to waste any time. Time moved slowly because I kept expecting a call from Mary. I anticipated the gratitude she'd feel when I told her what I had done about the death certificate. When she didn't call, I assumed she was busy taking care of all those worrisome, practical concerns caused by the death of a spouse.

I went home early, fixed some dinner, walked the dogs, and settled in early with one of my faithful westerns.

I had an affinity for westerns because I had a distant relative who came from a family of funeral directors back in the mid 1800s. One of the sons left the family business in Massachusetts to learn the new art of embalming. Supposedly, he did some embalming during the war and then headed out West. He ended up as a coroner in Kansas City near the end of the century. Someday I wanted to research his life and adventures. I'd promised myself I'd find out more about him before I was too old to care.

12

Tim McWilliams was already examining the skull by the time I arrived the next morning. He was sharply dressed as usual. Accompanying him was an attractive young woman with long auburn hair, a tie-dyed shirt, and a pleated skirt that hung to her ankles. Anthropology seemed to attract the "free spirit" type.

"You're here awfully early. Some of your colleagues will think you're out to show them up if you start work before nine or ten o'clock." I always kidded Tim about college professors who came to school only in time to teach their classes.

"Some of us do work for a living," he jabbed. "Mark, I'd like you to meet Heather. She's one of my graduate students, another strange one who seems to like old bones. I'm trying to get her interested in forensics. She hasn't decided if she likes the legal end of things."

"It's nice to meet you, Dr. Jamison."

"The pleasure is mine, Heather. So what do you think about our burned up man here?" I quizzed.

"I agree that he is male. The muscle attachments and the brow ridges seem to support that. I also believe he's white because of his narrow nasal apertures. Other races tend to have wider openings in the skull for the nose. As far as age is concerned, that's difficult. Since he's missing so many teeth, I'm not getting any help there."

"What about the sutures?" Tim asked her.

"Well, all the bones of the skull have fused so he must be over 30."

"Good. How else can we estimate age?" the teacher asked.

"If there's a rib, we could take a piece and look at it under the microscope. I don't know the exact procedure, so I would find someone who does."

"Excellent." Tim was justifiably proud of his student.

"Mark, I don't think I can do better than what Heather has given you, except I think the guy is probably over 40. That's about it. I'll take a rib if there is one and do some work at the lab. I think I could get closer using a microscope, but that will take a couple of days."

"No problem. Take whatever you need. Let's go through the bags and see what we have."

I rummaged around in three bags before I found a suitable rib. Tim never minded coming over to look at specimens because I always sent him back with something to study. He used every opportunity to further his own expertise and his students' knowledge as well. We were lucky to have him as a consultant.

Tim, Heather, and I went looking for Gus, finally finding him in his closet-sized office next to the x-ray room. I had asked him on numerous occasions if he would like to move upstairs to one of the larger offices, but he always declined. He said he liked being "close to the action," so I'd stopped asking.

"Gus, Dr. McWilliams has a few thoughts about the skull from yesterday." I encouraged Tim to discuss the case with Gus.

"So far, everything is consistent with what you've told me about the missing man. I'll let you know if I can get a better age estimate after I look at the rib. I should have something for you within a couple of days," Tim replied.

"That's great," Gus responded. "I'll bring Detective Ralfin up to speed. He'll be glad to know he's probably on the right track. Hopefully he'll have more information for us when I call."

"Contact me if anything important comes up. Do we have anything for today?" I asked.

"Nothing exciting. One case from the prison hospital, a probable accidental overdose, and some guy found dead in his truck after it went off the side of the road."

"Let me get settled in, eat my bagel, and then I'll be down. Tell Bill to put anyone on the table he wants first. I don't particularly care." I turned to leave and had my back to Gus when he stopped me.

"Oh, Doc. Did you forget we have the cops coming over today?"

"No, I didn't remember. I'll see what Karen has planned."

"She has to go over to Joplin on a change of venue. That guy who stabbed his girlfriend is finally going to trial."

"Okay. I'll be down about 9:30."

AT 9:20 I RECEIVED A CALL from Mary.

"Well, hello there." I hoped I didn't sound as ridiculously excited as I felt.

"Hi, Mark. I wanted to know if you were free for lunch."

"Absolutely. Just name the place."

"How about McGuire's? They have an oriental chicken salad I'm fond of. Is that all right with you?"

"Good choice. I have a couple of cases to do before lunch. Could we meet at 12 or 12:15?"

"I'll see you at 12:15. Bye."

I hung up the phone, unable to keep the grin off my face. I had tried to avoid obsessing about her yesterday, but I hadn't been completely successful. It was a relief to hear from her.

Down in the morgue, I hurriedly changed my clothes, anxious now to get started. I didn't want anything to make me late for my luncheon date.

I met Detective Sid Freeman standing at the table with four new recruits.

"Hey Doc, got some new ones for you. Do you have something real juicy for them? Maybe one that's been out in the field for awhile, or maybe one from a lake?" Sid loved playing with the minds of the new officers. At least one of them probably didn't want to be here, but my guess as to which one it might be was usually wrong. Sometimes the "macho men" were the first to leave the room, while women seemed to do a little better. They generally had the toughest time with the smell, but most of them usually stuck it out to the end.

"Sorry. Nothing too exciting today. In fact, the cases may be a little boring," I said as Bill began wheeling the first body up to the table.

I helped lift the body from the cart to the table. I glanced over to the observers and asked if anyone wanted to put on a pair of gloves and help, but not surprisingly, no one volunteered to assist.

The first case was the truck driver who was discovered dead in his truck off the side of the road. The interesting finding was the disease that had caused his death. I examined the outside of the body and asked if anyone saw any signs of injury. Because there was nothing visible, the tallest of the four men said he didn't expect the man to have any injuries because he'd heard there was really no accident. According to the police report, the semi had gone off the side of the road, and there was no impact except when the front of the truck had plowed into the embankment.

"Well then, if the impact wasn't serious enough to cause external trauma, what might have killed the guy?" I asked the new officer.

"Probably heart disease," he answered confidently.

I was pleased with his logical thinking. "I'd guess that also. We'll know shortly."

Within a few minutes I had sawed out the chest plate and was able to see the organs. I motioned the observers over for a closer look.

"Look at this." I pointed to the middle of the chest at the pericardial sac which covers the heart.. The sac was stretched because blood had filled up the space around the heart. As I opened the sac with a pair of scissors, I heard one of the officers remark, "Geez, look at all the blood."

"So what caused this?" I asked.

"He must have hit his chest to cause bleeding like that," someone guessed.

"That's a possibility, but I don't think so. Wait just a second and I'll show you." I pulled out the clot of blood surrounding the heart and placed it in a pan for weighing. The blood clot weighed almost 10 ounces. The normal amount of fluid around the heart was usually less than two ounces and it wasn't blood. I explained this to the officers.

As soon as I had removed the clot, I could see that the blood had originated from a hole in the front part of the heart, which I pointed out before I removed the actual organ. Cross sections of the heart wall revealed the hole was in an area of dead muscle. The man had had a heart attack a few days prior to his death and the weakened wall had finally ruptured. This was not a common occurrence, and I was glad the case hadn't been as boring as I'd originally anticipated.

The next case was not as interesting. A 36-year-old prisoner had died unexpectedly in his cell. There was only one significant finding during the autopsy and that was some fragmented white pill material in his stomach. His job in prison was to help out in the infirmary. The drug screen would tell us what he had probably ingested from the infirmary to cause his death.

I was finished with the cases by 11:30. Sid and the new recruits thanked me for the instruction, and I ran to change my clothes. I didn't want to be late to meet Mary.

We arrived at McGuire's at the same time. Fortunately we didn't have to wait, although I would have relished a little time to just gather my thoughts before we began to talk. For some strange reason, I felt a bit awkward, or maybe even shy. I asked for a booth away from the busy bar so we could converse privately.

"How's your day been?" I fumbled for an appropriate opening to the conversation.

"Fine . . . haven't done much. Morning isn't my best time."

Mornings might not be her best time, but she certainly looked fantastic to me. She was meticulously dressed in tailored slacks and a silk blouse. Every time I had seen her she looked striking, never overdressed or overdone as so many wealthy women were.

We both ordered salads and made some small talk. Mary seemed bent on avoiding any discussion of our evening together. Obviously she was feeling as shy about the whole experience as I was. I decided that business was the best topic of discussion.

"Mary, I've reviewed your husband's death and have determined that it was an accident after all. I couldn't be sure he died entirely due to natural causes so I ruled the death accidental." I spoke as professionally as possible, probably to justify my own behavior as well as to convince Mary of the reasons for the change in my ruling.

Somehow that was the needed icebreaker for the conversation. Mary's eyes widened and warmed, and she impulsively took both my hands across the table to thank me. "I think you've just saved my life, Mark. I don't know how I'll ever repay you."

I wasn't too concerned about repayment, because I knew there would be lots of opportunities in the months and years to come for her to express her gratitude. I was just happy to see her body posture and her eyes return to the vitality and sensuality of our previous dinner. The waitress approached the table as I was reveling in those eyes that seemed to always pull me in.

"Can I get you anything else?" the waitress asked.

"How about a glass of wine?" Mary suggested. "I want to celebrate." Alcohol during working hours was not my usual routine, but my life was changing so quickly, I was letting go of "old routines" without even thinking. I ordered a bottle of Chardonnay, hoping that it was sophisticated enough for Mary.

By the time we'd consumed the wine, I was convinced that I wouldn't be returning to work until tomorrow. But Mary's next comment snuffed out that impetuous thinking immediately.

"Mark, I need to let you know that I'm leaving town for awhile."

"Is there a problem, Mary? Is it something I can help with?"

"My sister Grace—you met her at the funeral—has invited me to New York to spend some time with her. I think I need to get away and think about some things. I need to figure out what I want to do with the rest of my life."

I understood her reasoning, but I was also strangely hurt. Maybe I was expecting too much so soon after her husband's death. Was it possible that the other night had no meaning for her? What could I say to her to change her mind? Should I even try?

"Oh ... I understand." Well, this profound answer certainly wouldn't let her know how much she meant to me. And yet my insecurities wouldn't let me blurt out how much I needed her to stay. She seemed so cool and aloof. "How long will you be gone?"

"Mark, I honestly don't know. As long as it takes."

The last few minutes of our lunch together passed in relative silence. Her lack of emotion was bewildering, but I could remember the numbness I'd felt after my divorce. Certainly the death of a spouse couldn't even compare in terms of difficulty. Knowing I needed to match her cool and dispassionate demeanor, I said goodbye at the door and she gave me a brief hug that I listlessly returned. I watched her car leave the parking lot, still refusing to acknowledge that she was leaving me.

13

The days moved on with exasperating languor. Work was my antidote and as experience had taught me, the distraction of the forensic world usually brought me out of any funk I was buried in. I had consulted on a case from Massachusetts about a year ago, after previously deciding that consulting work was not for me. I was tired of the traveling and putting up with all the bullshit from attorneys, but I broke my rule this time because an old college pal of mine, Arnold Aronson, needed some help. He had been accused of killing his 82-year-old mother and the case was now coming to trial. I had made arrangements for Karen to cover for me Monday afternoon and all day Tuesday so I could testify in Arnold Aronson's defense. She was happy to do the extra work, and Gus was willing to take care of the dogs.

Arnold had cared for his senile mother who lived with him for several years. Because she had died at home, the case centered on whether or not she died as a complication of abuse. She had a bad heart and was confined to bed, but her body had been found covered with bruises. Arnold was accused of beating her and causing her to have a heart attack. Though I hadn't reviewed the case lately, I knew I'd have plenty of time to do so on the flight.

Tuesday afternoon I found myself in the Springfield airport waiting for a flight that should have taken off the day before. The airport was closed due to thunderstorms. I had already spent four hours waiting, something I had little patience for anymore.

Usually oblivious to what I was wearing, today my wool sport coat and slacks were painfully hot, and the wool caused me to keep slipping down the plastic molded chair. The waiting room was filled with multicolored rows of chairs to match the tired gray linoleum. Advertisements of a local college and bank presidents welcoming the masses completed the jarring decor. The waiting people were irritable and disgruntled due to the delays wreaking havoc with connecting flights. I was sure my connector from St. Louis to Boston was going to be a problem as well.

I tried many times to read, but couldn't concentrate. I found myself scrutinizing the people in various stages of ill humor sprawled on the chairs and the floor throughout the waiting area. One of them, an attractive college student with tan, shapely legs and a tight leather skirt seated a few chairs down, caught my eye. Though she must have been aware that most male eyes in the room had noticed her, she never looked up from her textbook. Some of the businessmen in their pinstriped suits, who paced the floor and tried to surreptitiously glance in her direction, were also unsuccessful in prying her away from her schoolwork.

Why had I agreed to consult in this case? The flights alone would take most of the day and I would probably be picked up by some moderately attractive legal aide who would have been told to make sure I was comfortable. Of course she'd care nothing about me and would spend the majority of the time babbling on about her prospects in the legal world, trying halfheartedly to engage me in conversation, when all I wanted was to get to the courthouse and get the testifying over with. She might even feel worse because I wouldn't flirt with her like some salesman who had fine-tuned his small talk gibberish out of necessity to keep boredom from ruining his life.

The crowd was increasingly restless. Even the passengers who had been immersed in their latest trashy novels began to fidget in their seats and look around. The yawns and sighs of boredom broke the silence.

I walked to the nearest pay phone and tried to contact the attorney in Boston who had hired me, but he wasn't in. After explaining my situation to his partner, the attorney kindly said not to worry. They would put me on the stand tomorrow. I didn't bother telling him that I didn't want to testify the next day. That would mean another night away from home and the office and besides, I hadn't contacted Gus to take care of the dogs for another night. I didn't know if I could tolerate what always turned out to be a restless night in a strange hotel.

As I hung up the receiver, the public address system erupted into a crackling blare announcing that my flight was leaving shortly and the passengers must hurry to the gate. Why hurry? The flight was hours late and there was no way the time could be made up.

Eventually I caught a late, connecting flight to Boston. I spent the hours on the flight reviewing the case. The elderly woman had died during the afternoon while in her son's care. The paramedics at the scene noticed the many bruises covering the woman's body and reported the case to the medical examiner. An autopsy revealed multicolored bruises over the lady's head, trunk, and extremities. She also had advanced heart disease that the medical examiner diagnosed as the cause of death. He further stated that in his opinion the woman's heart gave out due to the stress of being beaten. Therefore he ruled the death a homicide.

The prosecutor had gathered, in his corner, both the medical examiner and a physician who specialized in geriatric medicine. Both said the injuries were consistent with a beating, and the beating contributed to her death. The photos of the injuries were impressive, showing large areas of bruising, especially on the shoulders and extremities, as well as the forehead.

The defendant had admitted that he grabbed his mother by the shoulders on more than one occasion to keep her from getting out of bed. He said that when she did get out she invariably fell, causing more injuries. He knew she was covered with bruises, but he didn't believe they could kill her or cause her any serious damage. The prosecutor and law enforcement didn't find Arnold's explanation to be credible.

With such strong evidence from the experts, the local prosecutor was obliged to take this murder case to trial. This case represented the first time someone was to be tried under a new law of geriatric abuse in Massachusetts. The prosecutor had a lot riding on the outcome.

The defense attorney, at a distinct disadvantage because he had to find a pathologist who would review the case, eventually found me. Many forensic pathologists didn't like working with the defense because they gained the label of "hired gun" or, worse, "prostitute" in their field. Unfortunately, defense attorneys were in a bind because the state always had an expert: the pathologist who performed the autopsy. The use of that person didn't cost the state any money. The defense, on the other hand, had to pay for someone to review the case, even if the consultant's opinion wouldn't be used in court. I'd always been bothered that the state had such an advantage, which was part of the reason why I originally did consulting work. In this particular case, I felt the experts had overstated the case in their zeal to have the first successful conviction for the new law.

After the plane landed, I heard my name being called and turned to see a good-looking, middle-aged woman looking directly at me. This lady was all business.

"Dr. Jamison?" she asked in her decidedly eastern accent.

"Yes," I answered as I extended my hand.

"Florence Anderson." She gripped my hand lightly.

I could tell by the way she introduced herself that she was anxious for us to be on our way. She didn't waste any time finding her car in the parking garage and then driving me to the attorney's house. I learned she had children at home and had to pay a babysitter overtime just to pick me up. She was irritated, but civil.

"Dr. Jamison, you'll be spending the night at Mr. Adams' house." I proceeded to object but she took a motherly tone with me and said she was telling me what Mr. Adams wanted. Those were her orders and she was going to carry them out. I didn't know what to expect and began to dread the evening ahead.

We entered a driveway off a quaint country road about 60 miles outside of Boston. My first impression was one of surprise. A small, old stone house built like a box was not what I had expected. I thought a successful attorney would inhabit a much more impressive residence. The home appeared to be at least 150 years old. I later learned it was originally built in 1825 and was added onto in 1980. We walked to the back through a well-kept flower garden and entered the house by way of the back door. My chaperon went in search of Mrs. Adams, who appeared within minutes.

"Delores, this is Dr. Jamison. Tom said I should bring him straight here."

"A pleasure to meet you, Dr. Jamison." Mrs. Adams was a small woman in her mid fifties who was dressed in a spring dress with an apron wrapped around her narrow waist.

"I have to run, Delores. The children need to be rescued from the babysitter."

"Sure, dear. I'll take good care of Dr. Jamison."

I thanked my chauffeur and she abruptly left. After settling me into a chair in the airy country kitchen, Mrs. Adams served me a glass of lemonade and then continued her preparation of the evening's meal while recounting a good portion of her life's story as I sat listening. She was a retired schoolteacher who volunteered at the public library and tended her garden of herbs and a variety of irises. She then took me on the grand tour of the house, adding to the history of her family's heritage and the origins of the home. Mr. Adams arrived during one of his wife's tutorials on her family's place in history.

Tom Adams was a distinguished-looking man with silver hair and a thin, athletic body. He exuded confidence in both his body language and his speech.

"Dr. Jamison, so good of you to travel all the way out here from Missouri. I'm sorry you had such difficulties with your flights. Maybe we can make it up to you. Has my wife been taking good care of you?" Mr. Adams spoke as if we'd been friends for years. His gracious manner and personal tone must have been obvious assets in the courtroom.

Over the next four hours, we discussed the case in detail. We did take a break to eat Mrs. Adams' fine country cooking. By nine, I was beginning to nod off in my chair. My host decided he had kept me up late enough and apologized for his rudeness. I urged him not to feel sorry for this weary traveler, and he showed me to the guestroom. Before retiring I made phone calls to both Gus and Karen, asking them to cover for me one more day.

The bedroom was similar to the rest of the house. It was bursting with an odd assortment of antiques that fit the aged home perfectly. I had never acquired a taste for such surroundings, but I could appreciate the sense of history that was palpable. On the nightstand was a book written by one of Mrs. Adams' relatives. The book turned out to be the highlight of my trip. Colonel Adams was an unheralded participant at the Battle of Vicksburg during the Civil War. The book went on to recount the colonel's role in countering a surprise attack by the rebels. If he and his regiment had not held their ground, the tide might have turned against the Union that day. The author seemed to imply Grant's future may have been altered had this attack not been forestalled. I had my doubts about this interpretation, but I did know that relatively insignificant events could alter the course of history.

The rain came down in torrents the next morning. Mrs. Adams informed me that they had endured 17 continuous days of rain. We drove the 60 miles to Boston in a downpour. My feet and trouser cuffs were soaked by the time I raced across the parking lot to the courthouse doors. I hated having to concentrate with wet feet, but concentration was the name of the game. I had to remember reports and depositions by physicians, witnesses, paramedics, law enforcement, and the defendant. I never knew what might be coming in the cross-examination.

As the first witness of the day, I quickly forgot my soggy state. The direct examination went as smoothly as I'd expected it would. Tom Adams was indeed the expert. He wasted no time establishing my credentials and my opinions. With a few short questions, he showed the jury that because the victim's bruises were of different colors, they must have occurred over a period of weeks. It was true the woman had a bad heart, and I agreed that she died of such. But to prove beyond a reasonable degree of medical certainty that she died as the direct result of a beating was impossible. I explained that she could have died at any time because of the severity of her heart disease. I also concurred that the bruises to her shoulders were consistent with the defendant grabbing his mother, but that didn't prove a beating. The cross-examination was next.

Fortunately for me, the prosecutor was more impressed with himself than with the preparation of the case. I knew he felt his case was so strong he didn't have to worry about my testimony. He was more interested in trying to make me look bad. But I had testified so many times that I was ready for anything this young attorney would throw at me. One ploy he used was trying to goad me into becoming angry. When that failed, he shot questions at me like a rapid-fire machine gun in order to catch me off guard. He also focused on my fees for the trip, implying I was the proverbial hired gun.

This inexperienced prosecutor was not successful. I was painfully aware that he needed to learn that expert cross-examiners rarely relied on such empty tactics. The best experts in the courtroom concentrate on the issues and the evidence, make their points, and end it quickly. During his antics, I studied the jury. Although I couldn't see into their minds, they looked like an intelligent group of people. I doubted they would buy into this prosecutor's histrionic display.

After my testimony, I was driven to the airport by one of the defendant's relatives who had business in town. We arrived with only a few minutes to spare. For the first time in two days, I could truly relax. I had a drink on the plane and slept for an hour. When I awoke, I relived the events of the trip. Even though it had been a major inconvenience, I was glad I'd made the effort. A friend had needed my help, and I was happy to oblige.

I was back in Springfield within four hours of leaving Boston. The dogs were happy to see me, and I was tired enough to sleep through the night without getting up once. The next morning, feeling refreshed, I hoped I would hear from Mary. Later in the day I received a call from Tom Adams. Arnold had been acquitted of his mother's death. I realized I had played an important part in keeping a man out of prison. Maybe I should rethink my position about consulting; it was a good feeling to have helped keep an innocent man from going to jail.

14

The intercom buzzed.

"Yes?"

"Good morning, Doctor. There's a Mr. Brower on the phone for you," Shirley stated.

"Who is he?"

"I have no idea."

"Well, let's hear what he has to say." Shirley immediately connected me.

"Dr. Jamison, this is George Brower. I'd like to meet with you if I could."

"Can you tell me what about?"

"We have a mutual acquaintance, a Mrs. Thomas. I need to talk about her with you, if I may."

I shifted in my chair. Brower... Brower.... Then I remembered. This was the man involved in the disastrous investment deals with Mary's husband.

"Is Mary in trouble?"

"Oh, nothing of the kind. There is no emergency. What I have to say, I would be more comfortable discussing with you in private."

"That'll be fine. When would you like to meet?"

"How about lunch the day after tomorrow at Country Club on the Green? Say around noon. You'll be my guest."

"I'll be there." I flashed back to 10 years ago when my ex-wife and I had been to the country club for a wedding reception. It was an elite club whose membership included most of the high rollers in Springfield.

"Splendid. I'll expect you then," Mr. Brower said with enthusiasm.

Because I usually didn't meet businessmen for lunch, I was especially intrigued as to what this had to do with Mary. She couldn't be in any financial difficulty since she was going to receive a very large sum of insurance money for her husband's death. Maybe her husband had owed Brower more money than Mary had realized. I knew I'd find out soon enough.

As soon as I hung up the phone, Gus appeared in the doorway.

"Doc, can I come in and talk with you?"

"Sure, come on in."

Gus lowered himself into the chair by my desk. I could tell he was upset. He didn't wait for me to give him an opening.

"I thought I should talk to you before Dr. Lipper did. We had a little discussion a few minutes ago, and I think I really ticked her off. I probably shouldn't have said what I did, but I can't take it back now."

"Well, what did you say?"

"Remember the baby case from last week? The one where the baby was supposedly wrapped up in the blanket?"

"Of course. You and Karen disagreed about the implications of the father's words. I remember you and the police were going to have another conversation with the father."

"We talked to the father again, and Dr. Lipper and I still don't see it the same way."

"What happened?"

"She insists on ruling it a homicide, and I don't think there's any evidence to support that. Even though we've talked to the father several times, his story hasn't changed. He still says the baby was wrapped up in the blanket, but nothing more. There's no autopsy evidence to call it a homicide. I know I can't make the call here, but this seems like a totally inappropriate ruling."

I listened to his account, realizing there had to be more to the case than what he was saying for Karen to decide on a homicide ruling.

"I'll talk to her, Gus. It's my responsibility to handle any professional disagreements. Do you know where she is now?"

"She's downstairs getting ready to do a case."

"Okay. I'll have a talk with her and see what's going on."

Gus rose slowly to leave.

"Gus, I want to thank you for coming to me. I know it isn't your style to complain." It was true. Gus wasn't a complainer, and it must have been difficult for him to approach me about a problem with my own colleague. Gus and Karen hadn't established a very workable relationship, due in part to each of them feeling threatened by the other person's closeness to me. I pondered the complexities of this small, interpersonal triangle and wondered how many of the world's problems were caused by similar vulnerable egos.

"Gus, I need to know something on a different subject. Do you know a Mr. George Brower? He's some kind of bigshot in the real estate business."

"Can't say that I do."

"I need to have him checked out."

"You want me to contact some of my buddies downtown?" he inquired.

"I'd appreciate it."

"Sure thing."

As soon as Gus left, I called down to the morgue to ask Karen to see me when she was available. She responded that she'd be right up because she hadn't started the case yet.

Karen arrived in a clean set of scrubs, clearly aware that Gus had already been in to see me.

"Sorry to interrupt, Karen, but I wanted to talk to you about one of your cases."

"I guess you've already heard what Gus thinks. I should have known he'd come running to you." The hostility in her voice set the tone for our discussion.

"Now hold on, Karen. Let's just talk objectively about the case."

"Why? You either trust me to sign out a case on my own now, or you don't. I've been doing so for almost a year, and you haven't interfered before." She was struggling to maintain her composure.

"Karen, I want you to sit down for just a minute and talk to me. If I want to discuss a case with you, I will. It's still my responsibility to make sure the cases are signed out properly. I want to know the facts in this case."

Karen perched on the edge of the chair and inhaled purposefully to calm herself. Discussions where she felt her expertise was being questioned were difficult for her.

"I think this baby was wrapped up too tightly by the father. He placed the baby face down, and he died. That means the father killed his baby. He even said he found the baby wrapped up. His lack of conviction during his statement indicates to me he knows he did a bad thing, and he's trying to cover it up. He wants us to believe that the baby tangled himself up until he finally just suffocated. I don't buy it."

"Karen, do we have any proof other than the interview? Is there any evidence besides the father's statements that make this a homicide or even a suspicious death?"

"I just know that some of his statements are suspicious, but I can't prove anything," she admitted.

"You know you can't rule this a homicide based on a feeling. The most you can do is call it 'undetermined' if you believe there is something suspicious going on."

"Mark, I know where you're coming from. And I know I don't have any proof, just my gut reaction. I hate to see anyone get away with killing a baby."

"I don't want a murderer to get off either, but I also don't want to fry some guy if there's a good chance he's innocent. We have to err on the side of innocence. Since there doesn't seem to be enough solid evidence to call this a homicide, you have to sign the case out as either a natural death or undetermined.

Why don't you think about it some more? There's no hurry, except to tell the police we can't rule it a homicide based on the evidence we have. We don't want them wasting their time. They're busy enough as it is."

"So am I," Karen responded curtly. She left the room without another word.

I watched her leave and sighed, disappointed that her ego still impeded her best professional judgments at times. But then who was I to be making value judgments about a colleague? I'd just signed out a death certificate falsely to support someone I loved. I was hardly in a position to throw stones.

15

The country club was a newly remodeled, 25-year-old facility graced with a series of glassed-in rooms with skylights. The brick exterior with its redwood trim and shake shingle roof gave the building an imposing quality of strength. I parked my car, glad there was no one manning the valet parking desk. Though I wasn't really ashamed of my somewhat unsophisticated mode of transportation, I didn't relish the thought of the sneer I'd probably receive if I had to turn over my keys. I attempted to locate the dining room. I thought I knew my way around since I'd been here before, but the layout of the main floor had been altered beyond recognition. I had to ask someone for directions.

The maitre d' led me to a table for two in one of the recesses of the simple but elegantly decorated room. A well-dressed man with slicked backed hair stood to meet me. He was trim, muscular, and over six feet in height. I guessed him to be in his fifties.

"So good of you to come on such short notice," Mr. Brower greeted me, as he extended his right hand. He motioned me into a chair on his left.

"No problem." I wondered if he really believed my schedule was that busy. I guessed he was being overly gracious.

The waiter was at the table in an instant.

"Do you care for anything from the bar, gentlemen?"

"No, just some coffee, black," I answered. Mr. Brower ordered a glass of wine.

My host began to pontificate on the exquisite wines the club had to offer. I just let him talk without interruption since I wasn't a wine connoisseur. After he finished his recitation, I attempted to ask about the purpose of our meeting, but he just waved me off. I sat for the next 20 minutes acting pleasant, trying to figure out why I was here and what this slick operator had to do with Mary. He had identified himself as a close, personal friend of the family. When I declined dessert, he finally got down to business.

"Dr. Jamison, I thought we should get together and talk about the death of Dr. Thomas."

"Fine. What questions do you have?"

"I thought it was kind of you to help Mrs. Thomas out in her time of need."

"She's an old friend, and I tried to be as supportive as possible. What's your specific concern in all of this?" I was abrupt.

Eluding my question, Mr. Brower went on the offensive.

"Let's stop playing games, Dr. Jamison. I know you signed the death certificate as an accident when in fact the death was due to natural causes."

I was stunned. Who was this man, and where did he get his information? I wasn't going to play his game, and I immediately pushed back my chair to leave. His words held me in check.

"I can see by your reaction my knowledge has come as quite a shock to you."

I put on my most professional mask, and responded with as much decorum as I could muster.

"Mr. Brower, I don't know who you are or what your motives are, but my official ruling on the death of Mr. Thomas cannot possibly concern you. While all death certificates are a matter of public record, the evidence I use to make my determinations is really none of your business."

He started to interrupt, but the adrenaline rush impelled me to go on. "I don't know where you get your information, but you might want to check out your sources." I threw my napkin down and rose to leave.

"There's no need to be hostile, Dr. Jamison. Let's just say that I make it my business to know things that may benefit me. You see, I'm a businessman. I take advantage of any opportunity which may come along."

"I don't have to listen to this." I tried to keep my voice under control.

"Dr. Jamison, I wouldn't leave. You should hear me out."

For some strange reason I couldn't leave without knowing what he wanted. I stood unmoving.

"I think that we can both benefit from your, let us say, indiscretion."

"What do you mean?" I still wasn't sure where he was going with this.

"Let's say the time may come when you could do the same for me. I would certainly reward you handsomely, maybe 25 percent. How does that sound?"

I couldn't believe I was standing there listening to this slimeball trying to play me. I left the dining room without a backward glance.

I drove back to the office, determined to keep my emotions and my temper in check. A flurry of questions were clogging my mind. Who did this guy think he was and how did he know about the death certificate? He was unquestionably a smooth operator, a real pro. What rock had he been hiding under?

While I'd worked desperately hard to keep thoughts of Mary from making me do anything stupid, I knew the time had come for me to break my resolve and call her. I'd kept thinking that if I gave her enough time and space she'd eventually contact me.

I didn't know if she was back from her sister's, but I assumed someone at the house would know her whereabouts. Her son answered the phone on the second ring.

"Is Mrs. Thomas back from her trip?"

"Who is this?" was his only reply.

"This is Dr. Jamison. I need to speak to your mother if she's at home. It's important," I said emphatically.

"Oh, all right," he replied unenthusiastically.

I tried to repress my feeling that Mary's son was a rude little jerk. I waited patiently to hear her voice. When she answered, I told her I needed to speak with her about her husband.

"Now?" she asked.
"Right now, Mary," I demanded.

MARY MET ME AT THE DOOR before I even rang the bell. With no words and little ceremony, she led me into the library. I sat down on the sofa. She offered no excuses for not calling me when she returned from her sister's. She seemed cold and very aloof.

"Mark, what is so urgent you had to talk to me now?"

"Tell me about George Brower."

After a moment's hesitation, she answered, "I told you he was the reason my husband lost so much money on the Franklin Building. Why are you asking about him?"

"He knows," I said.

"Knows what?"

I briefly recounted the highlights of my luncheon date with Mr. Brower.

"I don't understand how he could have known about the death certificate." She grabbed my hand. "What does this mean? Do we have to worry?" She tightened her grip.

"He found out somehow," I reiterated.

"Well, I certainly didn't tell the man. I don't even know him. Surely you don't think I had anything to do with this, Mark."

Her surprise and her anxiety both seemed genuine. Once again her liquid eyes pulled me in and the emotion I saw reflected there convinced me she was incapable of deception.

"No, Mary, I didn't mean that at all. Please don't misunderstand my questions; I'm just trying to figure this out."

"Mark, I know of Mr. Brower, but I've never met the man.

I know he's a shrewd businessman and has a lot of connections. Could someone from your office have talked about your ruling outside of work?"

"No one at my office would ever have reason to question any death certificate I've signed out. Everyone knows that my ethics are impeccable. This just doesn't make any sense." I felt slightly sick going on about my high ethical standards after what I'd done.

"Well, you told me yourself the death certificate is a matter of public record, Mark. Anyone could have read the report and questioned the ruling. Do you think the insurance company might have been suspicious?"

"It's a possibility. They certainly might look into a ruling that costs them double the amount of a natural death, although I've never had them investigate any death certificate I've signed in the past. Someone could have wondered about the absence of blood at the scene or inside the body and thought I made an incorrect ruling. But the person would have to know at least the basics of forensic pathology."

"Did you give a copy of the report to anyone besides the one I requested for my insurance agent?"

"I didn't, but I'll check with my secretary. Because the report is public, anyone willing to pay the copying fee could get a copy."

"I can't imagine why anyone would want it. What do you think this George Brower stands to gain by threatening you with the knowledge he has, Mark?"

"I'm not sure, but I definitely plan to find out."

And then the conversation ended. Instead of inviting me to dinner, Mary accompanied me to the door. I was dumbfounded by her lack of warmth. She acted as if she were a friend and nothing more. I wondered what had happened while she was away. Could she have met someone else already? Had I just been some momentary escape to assuage her grief? I had too many questions assaulting me to lessen my anxiety.

I put my concerns about Mary's feelings momentarily on hold and returned to the office, hoping to find Gus and check out what he had uncovered about the worrisome Mr. Brower. Unfortunately Gus was nowhere to be found. He'd been called out on a scene, and I would have to wait.

16

The next morning Shirley interrupted my bagel repast with the news that Mr. Brower was calling. I told her to tell him I was involved in a case and couldn't take the call.

I went downstairs to get my mind off Brower and found Karen already examining a body on the table. A thin woman, probably in her forties, with bright red fingernail polish and matching lipstick, was covered with bruises in various stages of healing. I glanced over my shoulder and saw Sheriff Lee Henry enter the room. Lee was an imposing figure at six foot four inches and dressed in western attire, complete with a white Stetson packed on his wavy gray hair. An old style six-shooter was strapped to his hip. He was the sheriff of a neighboring county, Jasper, and I had known him since he was elected sheriff more than a decade ago.

"Hey, Doc. Sorry I'm late. Got a little tied up." He didn't elaborate.

"No problem, Lee. It looks like Dr. Lipper just got started. Can you fill us in on what we have here?"

"This is Jill Johnson. Had lots of men friends. Drank a lot." Sheriff Henry was a man of few words. He would only expound on a topic if specifically asked.

"Where was she found?"

"One of her friends found her dead in bed. She didn't have any clothes on. Big party the night before."

"Do you suspect foul play?"

"Nothing really suspicious. Just wanted to be sure everything is above board."

Karen spoke up for the first time. "Sheriff, was there a question about the time of death?"

"Darlin', that's why I'm here. You guys are the experts."

Karen's voice hardened at the "darlin'." "Was she stiff when you first saw her?"

"I don't know. I didn't touch her."

"Well, maybe you should talk to someone who did," she said sarcastically.

I saw Lee perk up at the intended barb from Karen, but he didn't respond.

I quickly interrupted. "Lee, do you know who saw her last?"

"One of the boyfriends seeing her passed out at about 2:30 or 3:00 A.M. before he went to sleep. He woke up around 7:00 A.M. and tried to wake her when he didn't see her breathing. He called 911, but it was too late. The paramedics didn't perform CPR because they said she'd been dead awhile."

"I don't think we need to worry about the exact time of death if you believe the boyfriend's story."

"I believe him. He's so scared right now, he's telling us everything we want to know."

"What do you think about the bruises?" I asked.

"I asked around and most people said she had bruises all the time. She'd get drunk and bump into things. You know the type."

Karen turned around and looked at me. Without a word she stomped out of the room. I glanced over at Lee, who merely shrugged his shoulders, and then I began opening the body.

The examination revealed no injuries, and I informed Lee that the cause of death would probably be acute and chronic alcoholism if the drug screen revealed only alcohol.

"Doc, something wrong with your assistant? She left in kind of a hurry," Lee asked.

"I don't know. Probably just a bad day." I didn't want to get into the real reason Karen left in a huff. Lee wouldn't understand why some women might find him a bit offensive.

"Well, okay. I'll be on my way. Thanks for your help and let me know if I can ever do anything for you, Doc."

"Don't worry. You'll be the first one I call." I knew Lee was sincere in his offer. I'd heard this same offer many times from him and other law enforcement officers, although I wondered how much help I'd actually receive if I were truly in trouble.

I went upstairs after I changed my clothes. I was dictating the case when Karen entered my office.

"Why did you interrupt me when I was talking to that sheriff?" Karen demanded.

"I knew he'd made you angry, and I didn't want it to get out of hand."

"That bastard called me 'darlin'." Karen was irate.

"I heard him, Karen, and I'm well aware of how you feel about remarks like that. I thought it was best to sidestep the issue."

"You're just taking his side . . . typical. The guy's a chauvinist."

"I can't argue with that. But he's a good sheriff and I've known him for years. He would never intentionally be disrespectful to you. Where he's from, calling someone 'darlin' isn't rude. You're going to have to understand that not everyone thinks the way you do. That is, if you want to work in a jurisdiction like this. You've got to quit focusing on the worst in people."

"I don't have to like it though!" With that remark she turned to leave the room, but I stopped her and called her back. I was used to her outbursts. Her responses were always predictable, and I knew that time and maturity would soften her rough edges. I could only imagine how difficult it might be to live with a woman like her.

"Karen, I think now is a good time to have a talk."

"I'm not sure I feel like talking right now," she responded.

"I know, but hear me out."

She slumped down in the chair opposite my desk, a petulant look on her face.

"You asked me before about my meeting with the commissioners. You need to know that two of the three commissioners think we need to cut back because we're over budget. They think the best way to do that is to let you go. I don't want to lose you. One, I think you're a dedicated and conscientious pathologist, and two, I don't want to go back to doing all the cases myself. But if you start pissing people off, I won't be able to do a damn thing for you. I suggest you develop a change of attitude."

This grabbed her attention. She leaned forward in her chair and asked, "Why are you telling me this now?"

"Because I don't want you to do or say anything that might give anyone ammunition to support a proposed cutback or to force me to fire you. That means you need to please people, or at least not give them grounds to oppose you. I don't mean just Sheriff Henry, but all the local law enforcement and anyone else you work with."

I could read the fury in her eyes, and then all of a sudden she melted. She said with a softened voice, "I really love this job and living here. My family and friends are here. I don't want to leave. Have I really come across as that much of a bitch?"

"I think I have to answer yes, Karen. Is there any way I can help you with this?"

"No, not really. You know, Mark, I've always been a bit of a feminist, and I've had to prove myself my whole life. I've gotten paranoid that every man considers me his inferior."

"Just stay open-minded, Karen. You have a far greater chance of earning people's respect by being pleasant than by being a hardass who's rude. Your intelligence and your work ethic will win over your critics as long as you're respectful to them."

Karen seemed to take my fatherly advice in stride. Her smile was genuinely warm as our conversation ended and she left my office.

17

I had just returned from walking the dogs a few days later when the phone rang.

"Hello," I answered.

"Oh, Dr. Jamison. I'm glad to find you in. You're a difficult man to contact." I recognized the voice of Mr. Brower with chagrin.

"Mr. Brower, I don't believe we have anything to talk about."

"But I think we do, Doctor."

"Mr. Brower, I don't know what your agenda is, and I don't know what you stand to gain here. I want you to quit calling me and quit making your idle threats."

"I wouldn't be so hasty in your decision, Dr. Jamison. You should be very concerned about what I plan to do with the information I have." Brower spoke in a soft, controlled voice that unnerved me.

"You threatening me?" I questioned, starting to lose my composure.

"I don't know that I would characterize our discussion with that word, but. . . ."

I was thinking I had heard all this before in one of the old movies I was fond of watching. The problem was, this wasn't a movie; it was real life.

"First of all, this isn't a discussion. It's a very one-sided conversation that I did not initiate and that I have no interest in continuing."

"Dr. Jamison, are you still there?"

"Yes."

"I refuse to argue with you. I'll expect you to have a better attitude and willingness to help when the time comes. You have much more to lose than I do. Think of Mrs. Thomas. We certainly wouldn't want any misfortune to befall her, now would we?"

"I'm not going to listen to this anymore." I slammed the phone down before Brower could respond. My finely wrought nerves of steel started to crumble, and I sank into a nearby chair, too stunned to think clearly. I couldn't even sort out the chain of events that had led to this very unlikely scenario.

I was awake most of the night, trying to devise a solution to the Brower dilemma. I really had no idea if Brower could or even would actually hurt me. I knew I needed some sort of a defense if my ruling in the Thomas case was called into question, but I was inept at this kind of strategizing.

The best I could come up with was to secure a gun in case I was faced with a violent threat. Gus would be my connection for any sort of firearm. But other than that rather pathetic decision, I couldn't seem to formulate any positive plan to get Brower out of my face. Why did he keep bringing up Mary? It was almost as if he knew we'd rekindled our past relationship. But there was no way he could have known about our one night together; I hadn't shared that information with anyone. I still didn't know how to handle his threat. I couldn't go to the police because I had no proof of a threat. And even if I did, I'd be a fool to reveal my illegal behavior. I spent the rest of the night contemplating all the questions, but coming up with no answers.

THE NEXT MORNING, Gus and I sprawled out on the two easy chairs in the small lounge area next to the autopsy room. I was tired from lack of sleep, but the case I had just finished was exhilarating.

"What an incredible case. No arms, legs or head, but all those shots to the torso."

"It sure was," Gus agreed. "We don't see many cases caused by black talon bullets around here. One bullet would have done the job, but six? Those razor sharp edges sure do some damage." Like most cops, he seemed to love talking about guns and ammunition. He had quite a collection of firearms.

I thought about the first case involving black talon ammunition I had ever encountered. An inexperienced robber, irate because a restaurant manager came to the aid of his cashier in the midst of a robbery, shot the manager one time in the head and twice in the chest. No x-rays had been taken prior to the autopsy. I was fishing for the bullets in the area around the torn-up chest organs when I felt a sharp puncture wound in my right index finger. I quickly seized my gloved hand as blood welled up under the rubbery surface around my finger. The bullet jacket had gouged a hole in my finger.

"What the hell was that?" I'd yelled, ripping off the glove.

No one watching the autopsy had a clue as to what had happened to me. I stuck my injured digit into formalin to kill any germs and then placed a bandage over the wound. Returning to the body, this time I was more cautious as I felt around and found the first of the two bullets in the chest. The projectiles had black metal jackets covering their cores. Each jacket had been designed to open up into six razor sharp points, causing a large hole in the body's organs as the bullet passed through. The manufacturer's design worked perfectly, unfortunately for me. That was the last time I'd examined a body with bullets in the torso without having x-rays taken before the autopsy to aid my search.

"Are you okay?" Gus asked, bringing me back to the present.

"Sure, Gus, sorry. I'm fine. Just a lot on my mind. You were saying?"

"Those things definitely did what they were supposed to do," Gus continued, still talking about the case I'd just finished.

"Amazing, wasn't it? The hole in the heart was over three-quarters of an inch in diameter."

"I hope they find the guy who inflicted all that damage," Gus said.

"The deputy said they don't have many leads, but I suspect they have something. The guy was a Realtor and had only been missing for a few days. He was known to be a big time gambler, traveling to Las Vegas at least once a month. There are some reports that he was a wife beater."

"If his wife killed him, it'll be a difficult case for a prosecutor. Juries don't like wife beaters," stated Gus.

"Don't forget he was chopped up and thrown into the creek." The arms, legs, and head had been removed from the torso very neatly, probably with a high-powered saw because sawing through skin, muscle, and bone by hand would be both difficult and tiring. Someone had unceremoniously dumped the torso in a creek. The man who discovered the body thought it was a dead hog in the water. The head and extremities hadn't been located.

"I see your point, Doc. It would have to be a big, strong, and very angry wife to cause this much damage."

After a brief pause I decided the time was right to talk to Gus about teaching me to shoot a gun properly. "Gus, can you come up and talk to me after I change clothes? I've something I want to discuss with you."

"Sure, Doc. I'll be right up."

Gus showed up within a minute after I had arrived back in the office. He stood formally in the doorway until I signaled for him to enter. He sat down in front of me.

"What can I do for you?"

"You've been after me for years to learn how to handle a gun." I shifted slightly in my chair, trying to hide my obvious discomfort. "I was wondering if the offer still stands?"

"Sure . . . be glad to help you out. If you don't mind me saying so, I think it's about time. When do we start?"

"Oh, I don't know. No rush. Anytime's fine." I didn't want to appear too anxious.

"I'm pretty free this weekend. How about going to the range then?"

"Sounds good to me."

"Good. I'll pick you up around 9:00 Saturday morning. I'll call to make sure we can get an open lane. It's usually pretty crowded on the weekends, but the owner owes me."

"Thanks, Gus."

"No problem."

The request went more smoothly than I'd expected. Gus didn't ask any questions, and I once again appreciated his unswerving loyalty and his tactful reserve. Maybe someday I'd tell him all the details, but not now. I didn't relish the idea of confessing that I'd falsified a death certificate, especially not to my best friend. Gus probably suspected that something was up. After all, he was an old homicide detective, an expert at reading people.

The lessons went well. Gus spent the next two weekends with me at the range. I learned quickly and though I was not the best of shots, I was passable with the .38 caliber short-barrel Smith and Wesson Gus had brought for me to use. The gun felt good in my hand, and I became comfortable with it after just a few practice sessions. I was also glad the gun wasn't so large it couldn't be concealed, that is, if I ever thought I really needed to carry it. After deciding to buy one like it, Gus helped me make my selection from the weapons available at the shooting range.

During one of our sessions, I asked Gus if he had found out anything about Brower.

"Oh, I'm sorry, Doc. I made some inquiries, and then I forgot to get back to you. Sid Freeman has plenty of background on Brower. He's been around for years, a total sleaze from everybody's point of view."

"What's he done?"

"A lot. For starters, he swindled money from a bunch of local doctors, always good targets for investment scams."

"I know." I could be included in that broad statement. "Has he done anything lately?"

"I couldn't tell you. Sid hasn't heard anything about him in a while, but people like him don't usually change."

"Do you think the prosecutor's office would have any knowledge of his activities?"

"Maybe, but I doubt they would know any more than the police. I have a reliable contact there. I'll give him a call."

"Thanks, Gus, but I can call over there. You don't need to do this for me." I'd already asked Gus for more than I had intended.

"Doc, you're not involved with this guy, are you?"

"No, Gus. Don't worry, I'm just checking him out for a friend."

I attempted to brush Gus's concerns off, with little success. I could tell he was suspicious because I wasn't sharing any additional information with him. I was hoping Gus would let the whole matter go. I didn't want him to become involved in my unpleasant dilemma.

But Tuesday morning, Gus was back in my office with more information on the infamous Mr. Brower. He didn't have a police record, so he was definitely smooth enough to avoid anything ever being pinned on him. Gus assured me that the guy was dirty though, not just through his questionable real estate dealings, but also in certain drug and prostitution rings.

"Drugs and prostitution around here?"

Gus explained, "Mostly drugs here in Springfield. The prostitution is mainly in some of the larger cities. As far as anyone knows, he operates alone. They don't think he's connected to any larger organized crime syndicates."

Boy, that's a relief, I thought to myself sarcastically.

18

Surprisingly though, Brower left me alone. Unfortunately, I hadn't heard from Mary either. She was always on my mind and although I understood why she needed time, I was feeling hurt nonetheless.

Sunday morning I received a call from Karen wanting to discuss a case with me. She was at a scene and wanted to let me know what was going on.

Karen explained, "The fire department's paramedics responded to a call about 15 miles out of town. A man called 911 saying he had found his wife floating in a pond near their campsite. He said she'd walked away from their camper in the night to go to the bathroom and didn't come back. He found her the next morning."

"Sounds interesting," I said. "What can I help you with?"

"I'd like you to come out to the scene and take a look at the body before I have it transported to the office. Something doesn't fit, and I'd like your input."

"Okay. I'll be there as soon as I can. I need to take the dogs out and clean up."

She gave me directions and said she'd be waiting there with Gus.

As the dogs and I had a quick trip around the block, I wondered how Gus and Karen were getting along since their last disagreement. I also thought about how uncharacteristic it was for Karen to ask me to come to a scene. She usually liked to be the center of attention and for her to invite me was definitely a change in her attitude. The possibility of losing her job must have had an impact.

I drove down the county road until I saw a fire truck and Karen's Celica parked in a driveway. Karen wasn't there, but one of the firemen was. I recognized Deputy Albert Hodin by his size before I saw his face. He had played football for the university during the late eighties and his six five frame had filled out to well over 275 lbs. He lumbered over to my car as I stretched my legs.

"Hey, Doc, good to see you." His enormous hand completely engulfed mine as we greeted one another.

"Don't hurt me," I joked, as he gingerly released my hand from his.

"Doc, I wouldn't do that." He seemed concerned that he might have injured my scrawny paw.

"I'm just kidding."

"Oh, sure." He broke into a smile.

"What's going on out here?" I quickly changed the subject.

"Everyone's down at the camper. The body is just over the rise." He pointed towards the south. It's quite a hike. Do you want me to give you a ride down there?"

"No," I answered. "The walk will do me good."

Albert opened the gate to the field and pointed again in the right direction. The ground was soft in the rutted road, so I walked in the grass off to the side. After a few minutes of heavy hiking, I began to wonder if I shouldn't have taken Albert up on his offer. As I topped the rise I saw an ambulance and a group of people congregating near the truck's hood. A few yards away from the group, Gus was bent over what appeared to be a body on a blanket. I walked for another 40 yards before Gus noticed me and stood up.

Karen was with the group gathered at the ambulance and the three of us met at the body. After thanking me for arriving so quickly, Karen quickly took charge and pointed out the salient features of the dead woman. Lying on her back, the woman was dressed in a wet purple sweatshirt and gray sweatpants.

"Glad you could make it, Doc. This is shaping up to be a pretty interesting case," Gus remarked.

"No problem," I replied, always intrigued by an unusual case.

Karen began, "This is Laura Hatfield. Her husband said he discovered her in that pond over there." She pointed to a murky body of water to the east that could barely be seen due to its location at the base of an incline.

"The husband, Dorian Hatfield, said she was floating in the pond face down with her arms outstretched towards the middle of the pond and her feet still on the bank."

"That's an unusual position to be in after drowning," I interjected.

"I agree," Gus added.

Karen continued, "After finding her, Mr. Hatfield said he pulled her out and attempted CPR, but he couldn't save her."

"Well, that certainly sounds reasonable."

"Yes, but what he did next isn't so reasonable. He said he walked back to the camper." Karen pointed to a small, pop-up trailer camper at least 250 yards from where we stood. "He then brought two blankets back to his wife and carefully wrapped her up in them. He took the time to align the blankets perfectly to each other."

"I wonder why he did that?" I looked at both Karen and Gus for an answer, but they just shrugged their shoulders.

"After wrapping her up, he began carrying her up to the house by the road. He got tired and only made it this far."

"I'm surprised he made it this far," Gus chimed in. "She probably doesn't weigh more than 120 pounds, but dead weight is not easy to carry. It's not like carrying a sack of potatoes of the same weight. Besides that, her clothes were wet, adding to the overall weight."

I thought Gus could probably do it. I knew Deputy Hodin could.

"How big is the husband?" I asked.

"He's about 150 pounds, maybe five ten. I don't think he could've made it very far with her," Gus answered.

"Mark, I'd like you to look at the wife's back. Gus, would you mind rolling her over?"

Gus bent down and rolled the dead woman face down. Karen reached down, pulled up the back of the sweatshirt above the woman's bra, and pulled her sweatpants down, exposing her buttocks.

"Look at this." Karen pointed to a faint set of parallel, thin red lines on the woman's right buttock. Higher on the right side of her back was a similar pattern. Each parallel mark was less than a quarter inch wide, separated from each other by a pale area less than two inches wide. The pattern was like a railroad track traveling down the woman's back for almost two feet in length. The mark was continuous except for its absence in the depression at the base of her back above her right buttock.

"How did she get those?" I asked, not really expecting an answer. No one replied.

"They don't really have the dark color of a bruise," Gus added.

"No, they don't," Karen agreed.

I asked if she was found lying on anything. Gus responded by lifting up as much of the bottom blanket as he could to check the ground under her.

"There's nothing here, Doc."

"She'd have to be resting on something like the narrow edge of a two by four to get those marks. Is there anything else you want me to see, Karen?"

"Not really. We didn't see any other injuries except for a few abrasions on her nose."

Gus rolled the body back over after pulling down the sweatshirt.

By instinct, I bent down and looked to see if there were any petechiae in her eyes, but the examination was difficult because of the glare from the morning sun.

"Both Gus and I looked and didn't see any petechiae,"

Karen added. She was telling me my efforts were a waste of time since she had already performed the examination.

Gus pulled a corner of the blanket over the woman's face to give her some semblance of dignity. While he was doing so, I saw Detective Tom Ralfin walking towards us. He was coming from the south where the camper was located. Tom was an ex-Marine who was still in superb condition. His suntanned face and lean body were the result of many hours of running each week. He was a veteran marathoner, having completed more than 40 races within the last 10 years. At 58, he had the physique of a man in his thirties. I was not only impressed, I was jealous.

"Doctor Mark. How the hell are you doing? I didn't expect to see you out here. To what do we owe this honor?" Tom nodded to Gus and Karen. His actions indicated he had already spoken to them.

"Just came to help you with your job," I kidded as we shook hands. "What do you think is going on here?"

"I'm not exactly sure, but I know the husband isn't telling us the whole truth. You folks mind taking a walk with me?"

He led as we trailed behind, making our way through the grass towards the pond. The cuffs of my trousers were soaked before we arrived at our destination. We stopped less than 10 feet from the pond's edge. The land sloped down sharply from where we stood to the water that was at least three feet below us. It was obvious to me the man would have had a difficult time carrying his dead wife up the bank. I asked Tom if this was where the husband said he had found his wife.

"He couldn't give us an exact location, but he felt this was close."

DEADLY DECEIT

"Seems strange the grass isn't torn up except where we've been walking. Were there any shoeprints near the water or anywhere else?" I asked.

"No, didn't see any."

All of us were silent for a moment. Each of us seemed to be contemplating the meaning of what we were seeing, or more importantly, what we weren't seeing.

"Let me take you down to the camper." Tom began walking in a southerly direction.

The camper was a stand-alone unit that extended to about fourteen by seven feet when unfolded. The canvas top reached to about eight feet in the air.

"How did the camper get here?" I asked.

Tom explained that the owner of the house by the highway was the dead woman's uncle. He had pulled the camper down to this spot a couple of days before the couple arrived from their home in Kansas City. They drove their car to within about a hundred yards from the camper and then had to carry their supplies the rest of the way. Their car was gone now. The husband drove it to the sheriff's department where he said he'd wait for me to talk to him.

We walked around to the other side of the camper and I saw a shallow lake that was less than 25 feet away. As we rounded the corner, we met the other member of the investigative team, Detective Bill Jenkins.

Bill was the physical opposite of Tom. He was short and squat with a head like a cue ball. His rumpled suit and protruding belly were in sharp contrast to Tom's well-honed physique. He had an unfiltered Camel hanging from the corner of his mouth, part of his two-pack-a-day habit.

"Hey, Doc, nice to see you. Let me show you around this palace of country living."

One at a time we climbed the step and peered around the inside of the camper. The small living space was in the typical state of disorderliness as befitted a weekend campsite.

"We did find one interesting thing," Bill stated.

He lifted up the blanket on the bed to reveal a wet spot on the sheet that was at least 15 inches in diameter.

"The woman left the camper to go to the bathroom. Did the husband wet the bed?"

"We're not sure," Tom said. "That's one of many questions I have to discuss with our young husband. When I leave here I'll be going to the station to talk to him."

"I do need to show you something else," Bill added.

We all assembled by the door, and Bill led us around to the other side of the camper. He pointed up toward the body. I could just make out the top of the ambulance that was parked nearby.

"Do you see anything?" Bill asked.

Gus was the first to respond. "Some of the grass is knocked down."

"Correct," Tom announced.

I then saw what Gus had seen. There was a poorly formed path of bent grass leading from the camper to the body. I walked along the first few yards of the path and saw a partially exposed tire mark in the soft dirt between some clumps of grass.

"What caused this?"

"Let me show you." Bill led us to the overhang at the end of the camper and told us to look. Lying on the ground was a dolly consisting of a metal frame and two tires.

"Why would they have a dolly? They weren't moving a refrigerator or a stove out here," Karen asked.

"According to the husband, he used it to move some blankets and food from the car to the camper," Bill answered. Without getting too close, I scrutinized the tires.

Tom read my mind. "I think we'll be able to prove the tires on the dolly made the tracks in the dirt."

Bill didn't have anything more to show us. He said the family's cell phone was found in the camper, and it was in good working condition.

Karen asked Tom why the husband didn't use the cell phone in the camper to call for help.

"That's another question we need to ask the husband," Tom answered.

"Anything else?" I asked Tom and Bill.

"Nothing from us," they answered.

We thanked them for the tour and walked back to the body. Out of courtesy, I asked Karen if she minded me stopping by to watch her perform the autopsy.

"Not at all. I'll do it about 1:30."

An ATV was making its way toward us as the three of us returned to the body. Deputy Hodin was driving. I smiled, seeing his huge frame dwarf the machine.

"Care for a ride?" the deputy asked.

"That would be great," I responded. Karen and I climbed aboard. Gus said he wanted to stay behind awhile. I think he wanted to bullshit with Tom and Bill. Once a cop, always a cop.

I started to get into my car when Karen asked if she could talk to me.

"Sure, what's up?"

"I need to bring you up to date on the baby case."

"Go ahead." I wasn't looking forward to another tirade over this case.

"We haven't received any new information, and I think Gus was on the right track," she admitted quietly.

"So, how are you going to rule it?"

"I think I should sign it out as a natural death. There just isn't anything else I can do with it."

"Karen, I think you're making the right decision. I know your instinct is telling you that father somehow hurt his child, but you have to rule based on the evidence you have."

"I'll see you at the autopsy, then," Karen said as she turned to leave.

As I drove home, I thought about Karen's approach to difficult cases. I was pleased to see her making progress.

19

The telephone rang soon after I arrived home.

"Hello," I answered.

"Dr. Jamison. This is George Brower."

I wanted to hang up the phone without saying a word, but the tone of Brower's voice made me pause.

"I am not playing games, Dr. Jamison. I think you should hear me out." His cold, matter-of-fact voice instantly seized my attention.

"What do you mean?"

"I don't believe you would want anything to happen to someone you care about. This is purely a business proposition. I'm not suggesting you do anything that would hurt someone directly. I do believe we can help each other."

Now he was threatening physical harm. Was he referring

to Mary? Who besides my ex-wife and the people I work with was he threatening to hurt?

"I told you before. I'm not about to do something that is against the law. Why do you keep calling me?"

"But Doctor, you've already broken the law. I'm only suggesting that you do something for me and I in turn can do something for you."

"We've had this conversation before, and I told you I'm not going to participate in any of your dirty little games." I hung up on the man for a second time. Was he making empty threats? I couldn't believe this man would actually follow through on what he was suggesting.

I grabbed a bottle of beer from the refrigerator and took a shower to calm down and remove some of the sweat from the campsite scene. But I couldn't get Brower's voice out of my mind. The beer and warm shower eventually relaxed me enough that I drifted off to sleep while reading my favorite author. I woke to Mort licking my right hand, which was draped over the side of the bed. I looked at my watch: 1:15. I hustled to get dressed and by the time I had finished, both dogs were whining anxiously. It had been hours since I had taken them out, and they were dancing around my bed with full bladders. Our walk was a quick one.

There were at least 10 people in the morgue when I arrived a few minutes after 2:00. Deputies and investigators from both the sheriff's department and the prosecutor's office were all interested in this autopsy. Tom Ralfin was speaking to Pete, the crime scene technician. Karen was attired in her gown and scrubs, patiently waiting for Pete to finish taking the pictures he needed of the dead woman fully dressed.

Karen began by searching the body for any trace evidence such as hairs or fibers. The only strange hairs expected would probably be the husband's. Fibers were another matter. She could have plenty on her body from the camper and the blankets in which she was wrapped. Karen collected a few fibers from the woman's wet sweatshirt. The clothing was removed and each piece was bagged separately in a brown paper bag. No trace evidence was discovered on the naked body.

There were isolated injuries of the body that hadn't been observed out in the field. A few minor abrasions were present on the knees and the back of the neck. The scrapes on her nose were a little more obvious now that the body had dried out.

Pete took a flurry of photographs after two unexpected findings. One was the discovery of a twig in the woman's mouth. We all wondered why there was a twig still in her mouth when the husband had said he attempted CPR. Wouldn't he have removed it if he were blowing air into her mouth?

The other even more surprising finding was the presence of petechiae in the woman's eyes. All of us had missed these small hemorrhages on the inside of her lower eyelids. There was also mud in her airway.

"What do you think?" Karen was asking me for assistance.

After her request, most of the spectators inched closer to the table to hear what I had to say. I had to admit I enjoyed teaching people what I knew.

"These hemorrhages or petechiae are not usually present in drowning victims. The last two cases I've had in which there were petechiae in people's eyes found in the water were not the typical drowning victims. Both had been forcefully held under the water. One had her head pushed down from behind and the other was choked at the same time she was being drowned."

After the injuries on the front of the body were photographed and described, the woman was rolled over. I was particularly interested in the marks on her back that I had seen in the field.

"Tom." I interrupted him as he was joking with our morgue tech, Bill, in the corner. Tom walked over to me.

"Can you tell me anything more about the dolly?"

"The impressions we made from the grass at the scene appear to match the tread on the dolly. The lab boys will give their final blessing next week. They are also looking for some trace evidence on the dolly itself."

The marks on the woman's back were more obvious now than at the scene. The parallel lines on the buttock were a continuation of the lines on the back. Karen grabbed a ruler and began taking measurements.

"Each linear mark measures one quarter to three eighths inch in width. They are separated by a pale area that is one and three sixteenths inches to one and a half inches," Karen announced.

"Well, it isn't exact." Tom seemed bothered that the measurements didn't match up perfectly with anything on the dolly.

"It doesn't have to be exact," Karen explained. "It's not like you're drawing a pattern on paper. The skin is elastic and will give some, especially in areas that doesn't have bone underneath."

I looked at Karen and she met my gaze of approval. She could tell I was happy with the way she had responded. In situations like these, she knows she should be the teacher and help law enforcement understand basic forensic pathology. She was finally realizing she didn't need to be a bitch to get her point across. Appearing content with her change from adversary to advocate, she was on her way to becoming a valued member of the death investigation team.

Karen noticed another mark none of us had seen earlier. A circular discoloration of the skin, approximately three quarters of an inch in diameter, was located next to the top of the linear marks on the back. It was near the woman's backbone.

"I'm not sure what caused this, but it looks related," Karen admitted.

The rest of the autopsy was not very significant except for an abundant amount of dirt and mud in the woman's airway. This was a strange finding in a woman who was discovered with her feet on the bank and her face in the water. If she had struggled, her feet wouldn't have ended up on the edge of the pond.

After the autopsy, I asked Tom to meet Karen and me in my office to discuss the case.

"Tom, were you able to get any more information out of the husband?"

"No, he's sticking to his story. There is something about him I don't like. I know he did something to his wife, but I can't get anything out of him. I tried to press him for over two hours, but he finally lawyered up on me. We had to either charge him with something or let him go. He had such a smug look on his face when we let him go."

"So you don't have a motive or anything else to go on?" Karen asked.

"No, but we're checking him out. He's from out of town,

so it's going to take a few days to get some information. Can you give me anything for sure from the autopsy?"

I looked at Karen and nodded for her to answer Tom's question. I wanted her to take the lead on this case.

"The most impressive finding we have is the set of marks on her back. I think they were made after death because there was nothing on the ground under her when she was found that could have caused them. The petechiae in her eyes are also suspicious because they suggest she was forcibly held under the water. And lastly, I don't think her husband found her face down in the pond. It's strange that he said her feet were on the bank. I also don't think he could have pulled her out and not left any tracks in the grass or mud at the side of the pond."

"I'd add a few more things." I had to put my two cents into the opinion. "There was mud in her airway. I can't imagine how that could happen unless she had sunk down to the bottom of the pond. If she had, her feet wouldn't have ended up on the bank. The other strange finding was the stick in her mouth. I can't imagine anyone leaving it in there while attempting CPR."

"Since the husband has clammed up, we'll have to do a little more legwork." Tom didn't sound too happy about tracking down information on someone who lived over 100 miles away. "But don't worry, we'll eventually find what we're looking for."

I asked Karen if she had any more to add. She shook her head and the meeting quickly ended, each participant seemingly lost in his or her own thoughts of what must have transpired out at the campsite.

20

I kept thinking about the case as I drove home. The findings at the scene and the autopsy were very suspicious for a homicide, but the prosecutor couldn't accuse the husband of murder based on the limited evidence we had. Our prosecutor, like most, wanted enough evidence for a slam-dunk guilty verdict. He wasn't interested in taking a case in which the evidence was mostly circumstantial.

I parked my car in the driveway and headed to the front door. Strangely, I could hear only one dog barking. Sleuth's bark was much more distinctive, with a higher pitch, than Mort's. Realizing something was wrong, I opened the door cautiously. Sleuth ran up to meet me without her usual sidekick. I began calling for him as I wandered from room to room. I checked the kitchen, hallway, bedrooms, and bathroom with no luck. Then I thought he might have accidentally gotten shut in the basement. I opened the door to the basement, turned on the light, and clomped down the rickety stairs.

I reached the bottom step, surveyed the entire room, and found my dog. His dead body was suspended from one of the floor joists by his leash. I instantly felt nauseated and had to put my head down to keep from throwing up. I slowly walked over to him. His swollen tongue was hanging out of his mouth, and his eyes were open and glazed. I paused, not knowing exactly what to do. I had seen many dead humans hanging before, but never a dog, and of course, not mine. Numbly, I began to pet his still warm body. As I did so, his body began to turn around, and I saw the note on his collar.

There were only six words on the note: This did not have to happen. And then I knew why my dog was hanging from the ceiling. "That son-of-a-bitch!" I snarled the words to no one. Brower had done this, or had it done. This was his way of doing business. I think if I'd had my new gun and he was standing there, I would have shot him without thinking twice about it.

My thoughts of revenge dissipated as I returned my attention to Mort. I had to get him down. I tried to lift him up and loosen the collar from his neck, but I couldn't do both at the same time. Retrieving a knife from the kitchen drawer upstairs, I returned to the basement and cut the leather collar. But I wasn't ready for Mort's dead weight to fall in my arms, so he fell through to the floor with a thud. I picked him up awkwardly and wrestled him up the stairs. Sleuth watched my every move, whining and moving about restlessly, driving me crazy with her incessant activity.

I wondered what Sleuth was thinking, watching me struggling to get her dead partner out the door and into the backyard. I had decided to bury Mort under the maple where he had spent many hours resting in the shade during hot, summer days. I laid him down in the grass and walked back to get a shovel from the garage. As soon as the phone rang, I instinctively knew who was calling. I ran into the kitchen and grabbed the receiver.

"What do you want?" I yelled.

There was a pause on the other end. I think I'd caught Brower off guard.

"Dr. Jamison. You seem to know who this is."

"Of course it's you. Who else would call so soon after murdering my dog?"

"Now, Dr. Jamison." Brower's voice was all business. "What makes you think I would have anything to do with your dog's death? I thought you understood my position. What I have offered you is a straightforward business proposition."

"You son-of-a-bitch. What makes you think you can scare me?" Of course he could and had. I was scared now, more than angry. This guy was not going to stop with my dog if he didn't get his way. He reiterated that very point to me.

"I think you should be glad it was only your dog. I would hate to see something happen to anyone close to you, especially someone you care for very much."

His tone was so calm and measured; I could feel the rage bubble up inside me. I quickly decided I couldn't possibly reason with this man over the phone. I decided to hear him out.

"What do you have in mind?"

"Now that's more like it, Doctor." He paused. "There was

a young woman discovered dead in a pond yesterday. Maybe you know which case I'm referring to."

Naturally I knew. But how could he be involved with this case already, and where was he getting his information?

"Yes. We autopsied the woman this morning. What do you have to do with this case?" As soon as I asked the question, I knew he wouldn't tell me. It seemed that the less I knew, the more control he had over me.

"I don't believe that is any concern of yours." He answered as I expected he would. The urge to slam the phone down was irresistible, but one dead dog was all I could handle for the moment. I had placed myself in this incredibly vulnerable position, and now I had to deal with the consequences.

"What do you want me to do?" I decided to get straight to the point.

"Have you made a ruling on the case yet?"

"What do you mean?"

"Have you decided if the case is an accident or not?" The tone of his voice was impertinent and patronizing.

"No, I haven't."

"Good, then you won't have to further implicate yourself by changing a death certificate. Rule the case an accident, and everyone will be happy." He was not asking me, but telling me what he expected.

"But I don't think that's possible. There are too many unanswered questions based on the interrogation of the husband. We talked about it today and the evidence seems to indicate a homicide." I quickly realized I had lapsed into my forensic pathologist teaching mode instead of answering this thug who was threatening me to alter a ruling.

"Doctor, you can save all the explanations for your fellow doctors or the police. I'm not interested."

"The police already know this is anything but an accident. They were all there, watching the autopsy." I needed to buy some time. I decided to stall if I could. "Can I have a few days? I'm going to need some time to pull this off without raising too much suspicion."

Brower was silent for a moment. "I am a patient man," he said. "You have one week to rule this case an accident."

"I'll let you know."

"Remember, Doctor. One week."

I hung up the phone and my knees almost buckled underneath me. I slid into a chair before I landed on my face. I had always been able to maintain my composure under stressful situations, but suddenly my life was completely out of control. My dog had suffered a sickening, western-style hanging, my relationship with Mary seemed over before it had begun, and even my rock-solid career, the one stable thing in my life, was balancing on a dangerous precipice. I didn't want to analyze the sequence of events leading to this point because they merely magnified my own stupidity.

Returning to the yard, I quietly buried my dog. With the recent lack of rain, the ground was concrete hard, and the ordeal took over an hour. Rocks in the clay contributed to the difficult digging, and several large tree roots further impeded my progress. The digging was cathartic though, and the physical exertion helped free my mind of everything but the business at hand. Sleuth had no idea why her partner was being placed in the ground, but she never stopped whimpering. When I finished with Mort's burial, I coaxed Sleuth into the living room. We both climbed onto the sofa and sat there together. I stroked her fur, talking to her about the loss of our mutual friend.

Around 10, I tuned in the news. The main story focused on the morning's case and how the woman's death was under investigation. Tom was interviewed. He didn't say much, but he did say the case wasn't closed.

For a few hours, I had obliterated Brower from my head while I grieved over the loss of one of my best friends. But now I had to concentrate and figure out a way to extricate myself from my own ugly mess. I came up with a variety of plans, but none of them seemed particularly feasible. I was running out of options.

Then it struck me. I needed to do what I did best, and what I did best was discovering how and why people died by putting together evidence from scenes and autopsies. That was it. During one of my autopsies I could find some evidence that would lead to Brower. The difficulty would be to find a case that legitimately could be connected to him.

I spent hours in bed unable to sleep, trying to come up with a plan. It was about 3:00 A.M. before I developed a plausible solution. I didn't know if I could pull it off, but I didn't have anything to lose. I either succeeded and saved myself, or I was destroyed by the medical licensing board for falsifying death certificates. I figured my odds for success were less than 50-50.

The solution would depend on my ability to place evidence on a body that would implicate Brower. The evidence had to be planted either before or during the autopsy. I decided it would be better if the case were Karen's and not mine.

There weren't many types of evidence that could be transferred from a killer to a victim. There were fingerprints, bullets, blood, hair, and clothing. Simple enough, I jokingly said to myself. All I had to do was walk up to Brower and ask him for a blood sample that would eventually lead to his being accused of murder. That should be easy.

The best specimens to covertly place on a body would be hair and blood. They would also be easy to recover and preserve for DNA testing. Then I had to get law enforcement or the prosecutor to think of Brower as a suspect. If that were successful then Brower could be forced to give specimens for the DNA comparisons. It seemed simple, but that was only in the movies. Obviously there would be many variables I hadn't thought of. What a fool I was. How in the world could I pull this off?

But the alternative looked bleak. Brower had directly threatened Mary if I didn't do his bidding, and I had to protect her at all costs. If I just packed up and left my career and all my loyal friends in law enforcement, there was still a chance that Brower would carry out his threat. It seemed that I really didn't have any other options. I had to play Brower's game, but I was going to play it my way, using my expertise just as he had used his. The only problem was how to get it done, and that I hadn't completely figured out.

21

The next morning I arrived at work with my usual bagel in hand. I had to keep up the appearance that nothing was out of the ordinary, a difficult task for me since I'd always been the good guy, never the criminal.

The first thing I needed to do was to delay the signing of the Hatfield death certificate, the case in which Brower was so mysteriously involved. I needed some time. Somehow I had to meet Brower and see what I could get from him. I hoped I could get Karen to cooperate in delaying the death certificate without her becoming suspicious.

I sat at my desk for almost an hour, wasting time before I caught Karen passing by on her way to her office.

"Karen!" I yelled. I startled myself by how loudly I called to her. She stopped in her tracks and quickly entered my office.

"What's wrong?" she asked.

"Oh, nothing. Why do you ask?"

"I've never heard you yell before. I thought something was wrong."

No wonder I was questioning my ability to follow through with my plan. If I couldn't even do this without acting out of character, then how would I pull off something that bordered on dangerous?

"Sorry about yelling. I'm not my best today. Mort died last night."

"Oh no! I'm sorry, Mark. I know what he meant to you. Is there anything I can do? How did he die?"

I wanted to say I found him hanging in the basement, the victim of a brutal murder, but I didn't.

"He became sick all of a sudden. I took him to the vet, but he couldn't figure it out."

"Did he perform an autopsy?"

"No. I knew it couldn't bring him back. I didn't want anyone to cut on him."

"You sound like some of the families we talk to. You're the one who always convinces people it's better to know."

"I know. I know. Can we drop this particular topic? There's another reason why I wanted to talk to you."

"Fine."

"Karen, I'd like to make a suggestion about the Hatfield case."

"Sure," she responded. Her tone suggested she was already on guard about me sticking my nose into one of her cases again.

"I think it would be best if we sign out the case as pending investigation."

"Why would we do that?" she answered before I had a chance to explain.

"There's going to be a lot of media attention about this case. We can stop some of the calls if we sign out the case as pending and not jump to any conclusions before Tom and his colleagues have a chance to uncover more information. I have a feeling it might take a few weeks to complete the investigation. The husband lives out of town and gathering evidence won't be easy."

"Sounds reasonable. Anything else?"

When I answered in the negative, Karen turned and left the room. I had anticipated she might give me trouble, but she didn't. I hoped the rest of my plan proceeded as easily.

I went through the motions of doing my job for the next couple of hours. There were microscopic slides of recent cases I needed to review. Other than a few routine cases of heart attacks and alcoholic liver disease, there was little that sparked my interest. I thought about what had happened to me in such a short time, and the mess I had gotten myself into. Even with my career on the line and losing all I had worked for, the death of my dog kept a knot in the pit of my stomach. My two dogs were my close friends. My ex-wife had been my soulmate, but she was gone, and I had naturally bonded with my four-legged companions. I tried to repress my emotions as I thought of Mort again. Even my feelings for Mary and what I still hoped we could have didn't replace the hollow feeling I was experiencing.

The phone's insistent ring abruptly ended my wallow into self-pity. It was Karen. She was down in the morgue and suggested I come take a look at an interesting finding. I slowly rose from my chair, the burden of all my problems weighing me down, and headed downstairs.

"Hey, Doc. Nice to see you today. You look a little down," Gus said with his soggy cigar hanging out of one side of his mouth.

As I passed him by, I said in an aside, "Mort died last night."

The cigar almost fell out of his mouth. My statement not only caught him by surprise, it was cruel and rude. I didn't give Gus a chance to respond. As a friend, I should have allowed him the chance to offer his condolences. I couldn't seem to do anything right at the present time.

"You're going to like this," Karen promised as I entered the autopsy room.

I saw the body of a fairly young, white woman on the table. Her chest had been opened, but her head hadn't been examined yet. Although I rarely see attractive dead women, this one broke the rule. She must have been a real beauty. I caught myself wondering how I could be thinking of such a thing when I had just offended a friend, lost my dog, and planned to frame someone for murder. My own behavior was a source of amazement to me.

"So what do you have that's so good?" I challenged.

"You just come over here and take a look," Karen retorted.

The right side of the dead girl's chest was completely filled with blood. There was also blood mixed in the tissues above the heart, extending into the neck. This evidence sent me to the outside of her body to check for injuries. When Karen saw me going over the outside of the girl's body, she smiled.

"She doesn't have any injuries. She wasn't in an accident."

"Hmm," I thought for a moment, but couldn't quickly come up with a reason why this girl had bled to death internally.

"Care to look around the rest of the organs?" Karen asked, as if this were a game.

I was about ready to tell Karen I wasn't in the mood to play, but I felt compelled to try to figure out what was going on. I looked at the other organs. The heart was still in its protective sac and had not been examined, so that couldn't be it, and the abdominal cavity was free of blood, so the cause of the hemorrhage wasn't there. Then I noticed the girl's uterus was decidedly enlarged. I quickly checked the skin on the outside of her belly and saw the stretch marks.

"Has she recently had a baby?"

"Yes," Karen reported with disappointment because she knew I was headed in the right direction.

"Let's see. She recently had a baby and she now has a chest full of blood. She's ruptured a blood vessel. Ruptures of the coronary arteries have been associated with recent pregnancy, but that's very rare. You haven't examined the heart yet, so it could be a ruptured coronary artery, but I doubt it. Given the abundant blood in the tissues above the heart, I'm guessing that one of the larger vessels is to blame for her death."

"I guess I'll have to give you an A for that answer. Let me show you." Karen was relishing her role as mentor. She dissected some of the bloody tissue above the heart to reveal a rupture in the right carotid artery. Because this blood vessel is the main one on the right side of the upper chest and neck that takes blood to the brain, the girl would have died within minutes of the rupture.

"Karen, you've got another reportable case on your hands.

This will be an excellent one to present at the academy meeting next year."

"I think you're right."

"Don't forget to take some good pictures. I'd hate to see you have to use drawings again," I said, referring to her lack of autopsy photos for her recent presentation to the academy meeting.

Karen only nodded.

I thanked her for calling me down to see the case. I had never seen one quite like it before. Most of the reported cases like this one had involved rupture of the coronary arteries of the heart, not one of the larger vessels. On my way out I found Gus sitting in the break room drinking a cup of coffee.

"Gus, I want to apologize for my rude behavior. I shouldn't have said what I did without an explanation."

"Do you want to tell me about it?"

I told him the same story I'd told Karen. Lying was becoming progressively easier. He only asked if I knew why the dog had died and what I did with Mort's remains. He shrugged his shoulders about the unknown cause, but he told me he thought I'd buried him in the best possible spot. After he asked if I was okay and I said yes, he confirmed our original plans to go shooting over the weekend.

WHEN I WENT BACK UPSTAIRS, Shirley told me I had a call from Commissioner Garland; he wanted me to call him back as soon as possible.

"Dr. Jamison, thanks for returning my call so quickly." He was either a consummate politician or he genuinely enjoyed talking to me.

"No problem, Stan. What can I do for you?"

"I wanted to let you know there is a little problem with the budget. The other two commissioners are still concerned about the expenditures for the number of cases you've had during the past year." He sounded apologetic. Stan had been on the commission for almost 15 years, much longer than the other commissioners. They needed to make a name for themselves and were more interested in being fiscally responsible than worrying about the quality of work being performed in the county. I had heard that both the sheriff's department and the prosecutor's office were undergoing similar scrutiny.

"What are you trying to tell me?" The political process of county government didn't really interest me at the moment, and I felt no qualms about being direct.

"Doctor, I don't know if I will be able to convince the others that Dr. Lipper's services are really needed."

In less than a minute, I decided I wasn't going to play the supplicant to the political powers-to-be. My mind was focused on something more important than this minor issue.

"Stan, I'm trying to do the best job I can, and if your colleagues don't think so, then you need to let me know. How many years have I worked here with no major complaints from anyone? I'm tired of people not understanding what I do. I. . . ."

Stan interrupted, "Now hold on, Mark. We know you do a great job, and the county has been pleased with your work for many years. I just wanted you to know that we may have a few problems to work out."

"I'm not saying you don't appreciate what I do. We've always been on the same page, Stan. But I'm not going to crawl to your fellow commissioners. They know my budget is not out of range with other jurisdictions of similar size. If they don't like the way I run the shop, then maybe they need to find someone else who's willing to do this job on a shoestring budget. I probably need a break anyway."

I don't think he anticipated this particular response. He allowed me to finish venting and concluded with, "I'll try to work things out. Give me some time, Doctor."

"Fine." I knew I had unloaded on one of my staunchest supporters. I calmed down enough to tell him not to take anything I said personally because I didn't mean to imply that he was the enemy. At least the conversation ended on positive note.

After attempting to bring my emotions into balance over the next few moments, I decided I had to call Brower and put my plan into full swing. I really didn't want to talk to the man who was now merely the bastard who had killed my dog, but I knew the time was ripe to take a run at this sleazy operator.

"Shirley." I was in front of her desk. "Do you have Mr. Brower's telephone number?"

She looked up at me, smiled, and within a minute was writing the number on a piece of paper and handing it to me. My heart rate accelerated as I looked down at the number in my hand. I glanced back at Shirley and said thanks. The look on my face must have seemed unnatural because she asked me if I was okay.

I assured her I was fine, just a bit tired. I didn't tell her about Mort. I had told the story enough times that I needed a break from a repeat performance. Anyway, she'd probably learn about it from Gus later on since they were close friends.

After returning to my office, I plopped down into my well-worn desk chair and again stared at the number. It represented all that was evil to me, and my stomach responded with the same queasy feeling I'd experienced when I first discovered Mort hanging in the basement. That feeling was followed by an acid burn making its way up my throat. Maybe I needed something to drink in order to settle my stomach. No, I was just trying to avoid the inevitable. The call had to be made now, or I would put it off too long. I eased back into the chair, grabbed the phone, and dialed before I could chicken out.

Fortunately, Mr. Brower wasn't the person who answered the call. Now I could fortify myself for a few moments before speaking to him. The man who answered told me that Mr. Brower wasn't taking any calls.

"Tell him this is Dr. Jamison. I think he'll speak to me."

"Hold on. I'll check." The man had a gruff voice. I wondered if his physical appearance matched his voice. I held for a few minutes before the murderer of my dog answered.

"Dr. Jamison, so nice of you to call." He answered as if I were calling for a pleasant little chat. His cold professionalism was intimidating, but I was determined to match him. I refused to be patronized by some slick slimeball with no emotions and no heart.

"We need to talk," I said calmly.

"Doctor, you know what business we have together. I don't see any reason for us to meet. I think I've made my position perfectly clear, have I not?" His condescending manner incensed me, but I held my fury in check. He was also speaking as if his line was being tapped, and he didn't want to say anything incriminating.

"I have not misunderstood your position. However, there

are some issues I need to discuss with you, and I prefer not to do it over the phone."

"I'm sure you wouldn't attempt anything you might later regret." His statement, if overheard, certainly sounded innocent enough. Only I would take it as it was truly meant, a threat.

"I give you my word. And that still means something to me, regardless of what you might believe."

"All right then. How about meeting at the club again?"

"I would prefer not seeing you in a public place. I value my reputation in this town."

He chuckled at that, but didn't seem to take offense. Why should he? He had the upper hand, and all the power as well.

"I understand your position. Let's meet at my home where we can speak privately. How about tomorrow night, about 9:00?"

"I agree," I said, with little outward enthusiasm. Inwardly I was pleased. He had played right into my hand. It would be much easier to get the specimen I needed if I had access to his personal belongings. I felt a glimmer of hope as he gave me directions for the following night.

22

My car rumbled into the affluent neighborhood at 8:30 P.M. I was early. My throbbing headache reverberated to the beat of the country music emanating from the radio. Never before had I been so anxious prior to a meeting. My self-assurance, which I had always prided myself on, was nonexistent. Would my life depend on the outcome of this ominous rendezvous?

Lingering less than a hundred yards from the massive wrought-iron gate, I was startled to see it slowly opening. Obviously Brower's security system was quite sophisticated. Was he watching my every move? A white, late-model Mercedes shone in the dusk as it rolled out of the driveway. I couldn't see the driver through the tinted glass, but the car was familiar to me. I just couldn't place it.

My headache subsided somewhat as I clamped down on my emotions. Calmness settled over me after the details of the plan once again crept through my mind. I was ready; the time was at hand. I positioned my car adjacent to the intercom and announced my arrival to the faceless box.

"We've been expecting you, Doctor," a formal voice crackled.

As my car's tires floated over the glass-like smoothness of the driveway, I steeled my resolve to control my destiny. I parked, walked up to the door, and paused. I consciously worked to control my breathing, and I forced an exhalation to relax my muscles. I lifted and released the doorknocker, causing a resounding metallic echo.

A well-muscled hulk opened the door and led me through the foyer. The architecture of the place was impressive. We stopped in front of an ornately carved, wooden door. My guide slid it open to reveal Brower seated behind a large, glass-topped cherry desk. He stood to greet me.

"Dr. Jamison, thank you for coming to my humble home." His manner was condescending, but cordial.

"I wouldn't call this place humble." I tried to remain calm, covertly planning how I could gain access to the rest of the house to obtain the evidence I needed. For the next few moments I attempted to convince my adversary why I needed more time to make my ruling.

"I just can't rule this case an accidental death while an investigation is underway. This is not the time for anyone from the sheriff's department to question my decision. On the other hand, if I rule the matter pending, I have time to work through any questions that may surface. I've worked with some of these people for over 15 years, and they know how I operate. An early ruling would be out-of-character; someone might become suspicious."

"I can't believe anyone would be suspicious of you." Brower seemed to know how close my relationship was to law enforcement.

"That's true, but I need time to plant the seeds of doubt with the prosecutor. Even if the investigators think a homicide has been committed, the prosecutor won't take the case to trial if he doesn't have my ruling that it's a homicide. He'll follow my lead on this."

Mr. Brower seemed to accept my request at face value.

"You have two weeks."

"I could use one more. This ruling can't be so important that another week would matter."

"This woman's death involves a good deal of money, money that is owed to me. I'm not inclined to wait too long."

This was a startling epiphany. Hatfield had been killed by her husband because of a debt. Now I knew for sure her death was a homicide, but the information was useless. I had to bury what I knew.

"I'll give you three weeks." The statement was issued with such finality, I knew that to argue for more time would be futile. The meeting was over, and I hadn't accomplished what I had set out to do. I had to think of a clever ruse to get into the rest of the house.

"Mr. Brower, this may seem like a strange request given the circumstances . . . but could I have a tour of your house? I'm fascinated by the design."

The look in his eyes proved the question caught him by surprise.

"A tour? Why?"

"I have a special interest in interior design and architecture, and I couldn't help but notice the unique beauty of your home as I passed through the foyer." I couldn't believe the words spouting from my mouth. If Brower knew anything about interior design or architecture and asked me something in depth, my ignorance would be obvious. But I bumbled ahead and laid it on thicker.

"I rarely have the opportunity to visit a home of this quality, so it's a special treat for me."

He smiled slightly. As I stroked his ego, he lunged for the bait.

"I think that can be arranged." After a quick phone call, the bodybuilding doorman appeared. For such a large man, he was surprisingly light on his feet. My host instructed him to show me around the house, and I departed in his capable company.

We began by touring the rooms on the first floor. All of the rooms, including the kitchen, had been decorated with the best that money could buy. I caught myself actually thinking about the furniture and the accessories, and not about why I was here. I had to stay focused on my goal: finding an object containing Brower's fingerprints. The only other possible evidence I could use was some hair, because the roots contain abundant DNA commonly used for matching.

My idea of finding his fingerprints on some object quickly evaporated. With such meticulous housekeeping, there wasn't a single glass or any other object I could confiscate. I had to concentrate on my only remaining choice: hair. The downstairs toilet revealed no hair of any kind; it was spotless. I was desperate to get upstairs. Only in the master bathroom did I have a chance of finding what I needed.

After finishing with the kitchen, I asked my guide if we could go upstairs. The request caused him to pause. He didn't know if he could condone such trespassing.

"I don't know," he confided to me. His indecisiveness suggested he was rarely allowed to think for himself.

"It should be all right. Mr. Brower is justifiably proud of his home. Of course he would want to show it off," I said with authority.

"You're right. What's the harm?" He seemed proud of himself for making a decision. Little did he know it was probably the worst one he could have made for his boss.

My first stop was Brower's bedroom. I exerted some more control by pushing past the muscleman and entering without his permission.

The opulence of the 19th century fabrics and furniture caught me off-guard. It was an incredibly masculine room, yet it exuded a feeling of both warmth and wealth. Before the hulk had time to object, I moved from massive dresser to an intricately carved occasional chair, commenting lavishly on the quality and exquisite taste of each piece.

My enthusiasm must have been contagious, as the bodyguard ran his thick fingers over each piece that I lovingly praised. I pestered him with questions about the dates of various pieces, and his inability to answer caused him considerable frustration. Just when I had him totally confused with my queries, I asked if I could use the bathroom. Before he could answer, I glided quickly into the master bath and shut the door, telling him I'd just be a minute.

I quietly locked the door. The room was almost totally white and sparsely furnished with pristine accoutrements. There was nothing on the counter except for a gleaming soap dish. Speed was a necessity. I had to examine the drawers to look for a brush or comb containing Brower's hair. I needed to flush the toilet within a minute to keep my guard outside the door pacified.

I hurriedly moved from drawer to drawer. There was nothing of note except for a few extra toothbrushes and items like cologne and deodorant, for both male and female tastes. It was time to flush the toilet. With little time left, I still had to go through a few remaining cabinets.

The last cabinet yielded two hairbrushes, both containing strands of black hair. Which was Brower's, I didn't know. Just then I heard voices outside the door. It was Brower, and I knew he was asking about me. He tried to open the door, and when he discovered it was locked, he knocked. I grabbed samples of hair from both brushes and shoved the strands from each into separate front pockets as I fumbled with the door lock. I felt as though my heart was ready to explode, and I was perspiring profusely as I came face-to-face with Brower, inches from the door.

"Doctor, is there a problem?" He was polite but justifiably wary of my intrusion into his private domain.

"I hope you don't mind. I had a sudden bladder attack." I tried to sound calm which was difficult to do with my heart pounding in my ears.

"You don't seem well." Noticing I was perspiring, he must

have thought I was sick. He then glanced over my shoulder into the bathroom and surveyed his possessions, checking to see if something was amiss.

"I'm fine," I assured him.

I turned to my guide who was visibly distraught. My guess was that he'd receive, at the very least, a tongue lashing for allowing me in his boss's private rooms. I reiterated my gratitude for being given the grand tour, and I was unceremoniously ushered out of the house and into my car. My heart was still throbbing as I pulled out onto the main street. After a block I pulled the car to a stop along the side of the road, caught my breath, and waited until my heart rate returned to normal.

I headed home. Because Mary lived nearby, my thoughts involuntarily shifted. She was still on my mind, and I wondered how she was doing. More importantly, I wondered if she was thinking of me. Like a heartsick schoolboy, I decided to drive by her house. Two turns to the right and one to the left, and I was passing her home. I could just distinguish the front of the house from the street. I caught a glimpse of a white Mercedes parked in front of the main entrance. The car appeared similar to the one I had observed passing through Brower's gate. It must have been a coincidence. Surely there were many similar cars in town, and besides, it probably belonged to one of her friends. There is no way a woman of Mary's character and breeding could possibly travel in the same circles with the likes of George Brower.

But the more I thought about it, the more bothered I became. I had to find out whose car was in Mary's driveway. I turned my car around in the middle of the street and drove back to her house, parking covertly near the corner. The night was dark because a layering of clouds blocked the moon's glow. I glanced surreptitiously around, making sure no one was watching. I stole up to the house with amazing speed. Fortunately the light from the porch illuminated the license tag: MXN 6725. I sneaked back to my car, memorizing the number as I went. Tomorrow I'd ask Gus to run a check on the number.

My first action when I arrived home, after giving Sleuth some much needed attention, was to retrieve the bottle of Jack Daniels from the cabinet and make myself an unusually large and very strong bourbon and water. With drink in hand, I slumped down into my favorite leather chair in the living room. My nerves were less frayed by the time the glass was empty. Now to finish the task at hand. Using two envelopes from the desk, I placed the hair I had recovered from Brower's bathroom into each one. I was relatively sure the hair from my right pocket was Brower's because the brush it came from had a thick, masculine handle. The other brush could have been either a man's or a woman's. With booze making me drowsy, I quickly walked the dog and retreated to the bedroom. I was going shooting with Gus in the morning.

23

Gus was leaning against the doorframe, poised to knock at exactly 7:45. Seeing his shape through the frosty glass, I smiled at his punctuality. I flung open the door before his fist hit the wood. He was always on time. Our reservation at the shooting range was for 8:00.

"Good morning. You ready?" he asked jokingly, spying my wrinkled boxers and T-shirt.

"Give me a few minutes." I wondered if he cared that I was never exactly on time. If he did, he never mentioned it. I slipped into some jeans and a sweatshirt and made a quick bathroom stop.

Within minutes we were headed south on Highway 65 to the shooting range. Gus had his breakfast in bags on the passenger seat. Always generous to a fault, he pressed a gooey glazed doughnut in my palm and offered me one of the steaming cups of coffee. I fought to overcome a strange sense of lethargy.

We arrived at the brown metal building with its lone sign announcing "Mike's Range" to all who passed by. The parking lot was half full with about 10 cars. I began to feel at ease in this haven for NRA advocates and gun enthusiasts. I already knew some of the people due to their association with Gus and my office. Today was no exception. Sid Freeman was conversing with Mike, the owner, as we entered.

The building was not designed with comfort in mind. Serious shooters hung out here, some simply practicing while others needed to maintain their shooting expertise for their jobs. The only refreshments were coffee in a commercial-sized pot and a vending machine crammed with fat-filled snacks. A few old chairs surrounded a dingy metal table; the latest display of handguns had been casually arranged on a nearby counter. Mike didn't sell rifles or shotguns. He provided 10 shooting lanes for handguns only.

"Hey guys," Mike welcomed us. "You have lanes six and seven. Better hurry, you're already a few minutes behind schedule."

I told Mike I needed some ammunition for my .38 and he asked if one box would do.

"Make it two. I have plenty of practicing to do."

Gus aimed a quick glance at me, but didn't ask why I would want to shoot more than a regular box of 50. I let the unasked question pass.

Each target contained the classic silhouette of a half man on a white background. For 15 miserable minutes, I was unable to connect a single shot to the target's head. The next thing I knew, Gus was tapping me on the shoulder as I reloaded for the sixth or seventh time. I took off my ear protectors.

"What's up?" I asked.

"Let me see your target."

I flipped the switch and the target sped toward us. He took one look at it and told me to quit aiming at the head.

"Why shouldn't I aim at the head?"

"Look at your results. You'd have to empty your gun in order to get one shot to hit the head. Let's face it. You're not good enough yet to hit such a small area of the body. Aim for the chest. You have a better chance of making contact."

Gus put another target in place and sent it back to the end of the range.

With the advice of my mentor in mind, I began aiming for the chest. Wild Bill Hickok I wasn't, but most of my shots hit the target. Now I was in the groove. I kept imagining the paper man was Brower. Oh, was I having fun. I kept reloading and firing, and didn't realize the time until Gus motioned to me that our 30 minutes had expired. I was congratulating myself on my new expertise when I suddenly thought that such an attitude would probably get me into trouble someday. That is, if I ever managed to get out of the difficulty I was in now.

On the way back to my house I asked Gus if he could do me a favor.

"Sure, whacha need, Doc?"

"I'd like you to run down this license number for me." I repeated the number I'd seen the night before, and he wrote it down on one of the doughnut napkins.

"Anything important?" he asked.

"No, I just need to know the owner's name."

"When do you need it?"

"Whenever it's convenient."

WITHIN AN HOUR, Gus called with the information I'd requested.

"I've got what you need."

"That was quick. Any trouble?"

"Why would I have any trouble? The guys on the force will do whatever we need. Hell, we're all in this together."

I felt a pang of guilt as I internalized this statement. I'd already broken that trust with one false ruling and now I had to break the law to get my ass out of the wringer. I was depending on people who trusted each other, and here I was using them with clear-cut deceit. I felt particularly remorseful about lying to my best and most loyal friend.

"The owner of the car is someone you know." Gus brought me back from my self-flagellation. "The owner is Mrs. Thomas."

How could that be? What was she doing at Brower's house? She'd told me she didn't really know the man. Had she lied to me? And if she had, why?

"Mark!" Gus spoke loudly a second time into the phone.

"Oh, I'm sorry, Gus. What did you say?"

"Anything wrong?" he asked.

"No, everything is fine," I responded with little conviction.

"Are you sure?" Gus asked again. He must have picked up something in the tone of my voice.

"Everything is fine!"

"Okay then. I'll see you at work." He hung up the phone.

I sat at the kitchen counter in a daze. The mind can think

of amazing things when it's given a chance. And boy, was I giving it a chance. In the next few hours, I thought of every conceivable reason why Mary's car could be at Brower's house. But all my thoughts came down to the one theory I didn't want to believe. Was Mary meeting with Brower behind my back? Surely she would never trust him for any business dealings after what he'd done to her husband. I prayed that she was smart enough to know he couldn't be trusted as a source for borrowing money. The thought of Mary going to a man like Brower to ease her financial difficulties was absolutely repugnant to me. After I'd worked myself up into quite a frenzy, I decided I couldn't wait any longer to find out the truth.

She answered the phone on the third ring.

"Mark, I'm surprised you're calling. I thought we had an agreement that we were going to wait awhile before we contacted each other."

"I know that, Mary, but I need to know something right now," I replied emphatically.

"All right. What's on your mind, Mark?"

"I need some information about you and George Brower. I saw your car leaving his driveway last night and I need to relieve my own mind about why you were at his house. You told me you didn't know the man. Surely you're not involved in any business dealings with him, are you?" I braced myself for her response.

Mary paused, and then answered my question. "Mark, I've already told you, I don't really know George Brower."

"But I saw your car there."

"Mark, I have no idea where the man lives." She began to cry.

"Well then, why was your car in his driveway?"

"I honestly don't know, but I think it must have been John Jr."

"Your son? I don't understand. What the hell would he be doing at Brower's house?"

"Oh, Mark. The man is just horrible," Mary sobbed.

"Tell me about it." I was becoming more confused, although I felt instant relief that Mary hadn't been at Brower's house.

"John Jr. is in trouble. He owes George Brower a lot of money... more than $40,000."

"How?" The amount of the debt staggered my imagination.

"Gambling debts."

"Gambling? That's an incredible amount. What was he betting on?"

"Horses, basketball games... just about anything and everything."

"How long has this been going on?" I pushed for more of the details.

"More than two years. He only summoned up the courage to confess his problems to me recently. But does that matter?"

"No, I guess not. Do you think your husband's death has anything to do with John's relationship with Brower?"

"I'm not sure. I know that Mr. Brower preys on the weak and the vulnerable. Oh Mark, you can't possibly think that John had anything to do with Brower finding out about my husband's death certificate? Is it possible John Jr. overheard one of the conversations between you and me at the house, and told Brower?"

"Why would he tell Brower?"

"I don't know. Maybe he thought he could use the information to clear some of his debt. Or maybe he was just telling Brower about his problems, his father's death, and the fact that you had come back into my life. I don't know where you're going with all these questions, Mark." Mary sounded exasperated. She had stopped crying.

"For some reason, Mary, Brower must have used whatever John Jr. told him to then search the public records about your husband's death. I can't quite piece together how he suspected that I might have falsified the ruling, but he is using that information to threaten me."

Mary didn't seem as concerned as I'd expected. "I know the man is bad news, Mark, and you'll do well to just stay as far away from him as possible. I somehow have to help my son escape from his clutches, that's for sure."

I had no more questions about Brower since I'd finally figured out how he'd managed to weasel his way into my life, but I still had questions about Mary. "Mary, can I take you out to dinner sometime? I'd like to spend some time with you."

"It's too soon, Mark." Once again, a tone of finality surfaced.

"All right, I'm a patient man." She didn't respond. I said my goodbyes and hung up the phone. I felt somewhat relieved knowing that Mary hadn't been anywhere near Brower's house, but realizing that her son was tangled in Brower's web was a cause for considerable concern. First I had to concentrate on untangling my own mess with Brower.

24

Brower's threats made it imperative that I put an end to my involvement with him as quickly as possible. I spent the rest of the afternoon debating whether or not I should try to intimidate Brower with what I could do to him. If he backed off from his demands, I wouldn't be forced to break the law again by planting the hair. The reality of the situation was sobering. The man would just laugh at my inane threats. He was used to making threats, not receiving them. The only way out was to show him proof that I could hurt him.

TOM CALLED THE NEXT MORNING for a follow-up investigation report on the dead woman from the pond.

"Sorry, Doc, it's taken us some time to get information on Hatfield."

"Anything good?" I asked.

"You might say that." Tom sounded pleased with what he'd uncovered.

"Well, don't keep me in suspense."

"Hatfield has lost a lot of money in the stock market, almost $35,000 over the past two years. He works for a contractor, earning a salary of less than $30,000 a year. His wife worked in a day care center and made less than $20,000 a year. They lived in a rental apartment."

"So, where did he get enough money to lose so much in the market?"

"I don't know, but we're working on it. There's more."

"There's more?" I asked incredulously. How much more could there be, except for a motive? I still hadn't heard a good reason why this man would kill his wife.

"Life insurance. This guy has a $500,000 policy on her life. That's a lot for such a young wife."

"How old is the policy?" I asked.

"It's a combination of two, with the first one a little over a year old and the newest one not yet a month old."

"And how long were they married at the time of her death?"

"About 18 months," Tom replied.

I normally would have been excited to hear this information, but today I wasn't. The evidence was pointing directly towards an obvious homicide with greed as a motive. This wouldn't be an easy case to stall. Somehow I had to slow things down until I finished my business with Brower.

"Sounds good, Tom. Do you have any more work to do?"

"Sure. We're still running down other leads and hoping to find answers to how he got the money he lost in the market. This one may take a while. Anything more on your end?"

"I haven't received the final report yet, but the toxicologist hasn't found anything to speak of—just a little caffeine in her system, probably from coffee or soda."

After my meeting with Brower, I made sure the death certificate had been signed as pending investigation. Fortunately, this had not caused a stir, and the news media hadn't picked up on it yet. I could relax some. My reprieve allowed me the rest of the three weeks to find a case I could use to implicate George Brower. Meanwhile, I felt compelled to focus on my job; I still had to turn out the routine workload to avoid arousing suspicion.

There was nothing like a good case to get my mind off my problems. I had always possessed the ability to shut out any personal issues I might be concerned with when I had a case to do. I knew most physicians had this talent. Their personal lives could be going down in flames, but they still performed well with their patients or, in my situation, with dead bodies. Just such a case was waiting for me the next morning.

KAREN WAS GONE for the day, testifying in a gunshot homicide in Lebanon that was about 50 miles up I-44 to the northeast. This court appearance was only her fourth or fifth and I knew she was nervous. I remembered the first time I had testified in Missouri. A man had died in a fire near Ft. Leonard Wood in Pulaski County. The decedent was a known alcoholic who lived in a trailer. The trailer had caught fire. reducing the man's body to charred remains with most of his arms and legs entirely gone. The fire marshal didn't think an autopsy was necessary, but the newly elected coroner, a paramedic by training, thought one was needed.

I had begun the autopsy thinking I wouldn't find much except for the remnants of fire damage. But when I opened the sac around the heart, I found blood. I looked at the coroner, who was watching the procedure, and let him know that fire doesn't usually cause blood to accumulate around the heart. Further examination of the heart revealed a hole caused by a bullet. The man had obviously been shot. The body was then x-rayed and ten bullets were discovered throughout the chest, abdomen, and head. The coroner was pleased he had ordered the autopsy. I always wished I could have seen the look on the fire marshal's face when he heard the news that the victim had been murdered before the trailer had been burned.

The trial for this murder had taken place in the old courthouse of Waynesville. The atmosphere was so relaxed that I lost my first trial jitters immediately. The men and women of the jury were dressed in coveralls, suits, and dresses. I had instantly felt at ease. When I saw the man in the back row sleeping, I knew I needn't worry. I hoped Karen had a similar experience today.

I found Gus bent over the x-ray developer.

"Problems?" I asked.

"Oh, hi, Doc. This damn machine is acting up again. We could sure use another one."

"Why should we get another one when you're so good at fixing this one? Besides, the commissioners are raising hell about our budget as it is. I don't think they'll look kindly on such a request."

Gus only frowned.

"What's on tap for today?" I was hoping for something interesting.

"Can't you smell it?"

"You're not making my day," I retorted.

"You might as well go and have your bagel and come down in about an hour. The police will be here then. Sid is bringing some more recruits over."

"Aren't you going to give me a hint?"

"If you insist . . . maggot city in a ransacked house. Good enough?"

"That's plenty. The recruits will love it. I'll see you in a bit."

MY STOMACH was slightly bloated from the bagel and two cups of coffee. I walked into the morgue, where everyone was already assembled. The investigators, Pete Handler, the crime scene technician, and four new officers were ready for me to begin. Sid introduced me to the new officers. I asked Bill to bring the body to the table. He was in a foul mood, knowing what lay ahead.

The group began to grimace as soon as the body was removed from the cooler. Even though bagged, the odor emanating from the remains polluted the atmosphere. It was impossible to avoid the smell that quickly filled the room. Sid came over and asked me if we had any Vicks he could jam up his nose.

"Why would you want that?" I joked. Anyone who knew me thought I was somewhat strange for not putting anything in my nostrils to block out the smell. I was just so used to the odors, they didn't bother me anymore. After a few minutes, my nose became used to the nonpoisonous fumes. I always called it "nasal fatigue."

"Come on, Doc. Just tell me where you have it hidden," Sid pleaded.

"We don't have any." I was telling the truth.

"What do you mean?" I could see the disappointment in his eyes.

"We're out of Vicks, but we do have some peppermint oil that Bill picked up at the store the other day." Bill retrieved the bottle from one of the drawers and handed it to Sid.

"Bless you, my son," Sid responded.

Gus came into the room then, and he helped Bill and me transfer the body, still in its bag, to the table. I turned to Sid, wanting to tell him to go lightly with the peppermint oil and not get it on his skin, but I was too late. He had liberally doused the inside of his mask with the substance and now was paying the price. He ripped off the mask, complaining that his skin was on fire.

"Go wash your face. That stuff really causes a burn." Following my advice, he ran to the sink in the lounge. When we saw him next, his face was red and chapped. Determined not to use anything to stifle the smell, he pouted for the rest of the examination.

As the body was removed from the bag, the flies began to swarm. We broke out the repellent to keep them from proliferating. The electric bug lamp in the corner of the room began its periodic zapping of each new insect that was attracted to the light. We also sprayed our poison into the dead man's face where hundreds of maggots were seething from his nose, mouth, and eye sockets. There were a number of "ohs" and "ahs" and "that's disgusting" from around the room. I thought this was kind of funny given the number of macho men assembled for the case.

"Sid, what kind of case do we have here? I doubt you'd be here if you thought this was a natural death."

Sid became all business and recited the case and his concerns. The man had lived in a trailer filled with bags of trash and turned over chairs. The domicile was locked when the family came over to check on the victim. They hadn't heard from him in about 10 days. Since the man was a recluse, they hadn't been overly concerned until a week had passed.

"So, you think this man was assaulted?" I asked.

"I don't know. There was some blood on one of the walls and a few spots on the floor. I don't think there was a robbery because his wallet was on the dresser and it was still full of money. A bunch of guns hadn't been touched. Most robbers would have taken the money and the guns."

"Where was he found?"

Sid extracted some Polaroid snapshots from his folder and showed them to me. The man was lying in a hallway. His torso was bent in a distorted posture with his left arm underneath his twisted legs.

"The way his body is positioned indicates he dropped suddenly. This isn't the kind of position someone would be in if he were beaten and subsequently died."

"I agree," said Sid, "but I have to make sure. I'm hoping the autopsy will show he wasn't murdered."

"So do I."

The examination didn't take long once the body was undressed, and the maggots were cleared away from the face. He could have had some injuries to the face, but the degree of decomposition caused by the insects prevented an adequate evaluation.

There was an inch-long laceration on the left side of the head above his ear. I waited for Pete to take as many photographs as he needed, and then I proceeded. There was some hemorrhage under the scalp associated with the ragged skin tear. However, there were no injuries to the bone or the brain. The brain was intact. Some postmortem liquefaction of the brain substance had taken place.

"I don't think the laceration means much. He probably got it when he fell to the floor and bumped his head," I explained. "What kind of medical history did you get?"

"I have that," Gus piped in. "He had some heart disease and he was a diabetic, although he wasn't taking insulin. Other than that he was okay. His doctor didn't have much else to say because he hadn't seen the man in over six months."

The remainder of the autopsy gave us the answer we were looking for. The man had an enlarged heart and some kidney disease, both clearly associated with high blood pressure. There were no old or recent heart attacks.

There were no questions from the group of recruits. Most of them were standing so far away from the table they couldn't see anything. It appeared to me they were quite disgusted with the smell and the examination.

"I think he died a natural death, probably due to heart disease. Of course, I can't rule out drugs in his system, but I won't know that until the tests have been performed. Unless he's been poisoned, I don't believe there is anything suspicious. The scene also supports this."

"That's all we needed to know." Pete and Sid slid out the door with the new recruits before I even realized they were gone, obviously in a hurry to vacate the obnoxious surroundings.

My only other case for the day was a three-month-old baby girl who had died while sleeping with her parents in their bed. Clearly one of the parents had rolled over on her because the upper part of her body from the chest to the face was dark red, almost purple. The lower part of the body was pale. The dark discoloration was the result of being squashed by a heavy weight.

I didn't relish speaking to the child's parents after I finished the examination. When I talked to the mother on the phone, she was crying. Her reaction intensified when I told her that, in my opinion, someone had accidentally suffocated her baby in bed. Unfortunately, given the circumstances, it had to have been either her or her husband. I knew the guilt of this tragic accident would stay with them forever.

25

The days passed slowly. Almost two weeks went by before I was able to put my plan into effect. The body of a young woman had been brought into the office the previous night. She was found in an alley, obviously dumped there because there were no signs of a struggle or blood at the scene. Dressed in a short, tight, black dress and no shoes, she had a few bruises on her neck and appeared as if she'd been struck a few times about the face. I had heard that her body had been discovered less than a block from the Franklin Building, the building that had contributed to the Thomas's financial woes. I thought the nearness of the dead woman's body to Brower's building might work to my advantage.

The body was already on the table when I came into the morgue, but no one else was around. I needed to work fast before anyone joined me. Karen was probably changing her clothes. I quickly reached into my shirt pocket and grabbed the envelopes I had brought to work each morning, waiting for just such an opportunity. Inside was the hair I had taken from Brower's bathroom. I removed some of the hair from each envelope and placed them on the body. I deposited at least one strand from each on the neck, a couple on her right hand, and several on her abdomen and pubic hair under her dress. Not surprisingly, she wasn't wearing any panties.

I knew Karen would find these planted specimens because she was a meticulous examiner. Gus, Bill, Sid, and Pete Handler were talking loudly and joking as they entered the room with Karen. Sid was the first to greet me.

"Good morning, Doc. I think I'm seeing a little too much of you lately. At least this one doesn't stink. Hey, I didn't think you were on this case."

"I'm not," I said nervously, "I wanted to see what was happening. I heard it might be an interesting case. Care to tell me about it?"

"Looks like someone knocked off one of the ladies of the evening."

"How do you know her so well, Sid?" I kidded.

"No personal knowledge," he was quick to respond. "We really didn't know her; she's not from around here. We printed her last night and discovered she has quite a record, including a bunch of arrests for prostitution in St. Louis."

"She must be high class. She looks pretty good."

"Yeah, for a dead girl," Sid countered.

"Touché."

As I suspected, Karen did a very thorough examination. She recovered all of the hairs I had planted, and everyone was pleased that so much evidence was discovered. In most cases, the yield of evidence is low. Karen performed a sexual assault kit. She took oral, anal, and vaginal swabs, pubic hair combings, and samples of head and pubic hair. Blood was taken for DNA comparisons if needed.

While Karen was collecting the vaginal swabs, I began to realize my plan had one major flaw. If the woman's vaginal swab contained semen, that DNA wouldn't match up with the DNA of the planted hairs. That would be discovered, however, only if the DNA of the hair was checked. It wouldn't be high on the lab's list for testing if DNA could be obtained from the semen specimen. I thought I'd deal with that later if I had to.

"Mark, you might as well look at this," Karen said. She had exposed the dead girl's eyes to reveal pinpoint hemorrhages.

"Those and the bruises on her neck sure do make it look like a strangulation," I stated.

"They certainly do," Karen agreed, "but I don't want to jump to any conclusions before I look on the inside."

I wanted to say "good girl" for her answer, but that wouldn't be something I could get away with in mixed company.

Karen did find bleeding deep within the neck tissues and a broken hyoid. She knew that a broken hyoid bone was almost a sure sign of manual strangulation. The assailant's thumbs usually broke the bone as pressure was applied to the neck. She explained all this to Sid.

Pete was the person who received the rape kit and the hairs

and was responsible for delivering them to the lab. He made sure the chain-of-custody forms were filled out correctly so no defense attorney could have the evidence thrown out on some technicality.

After Karen had completed her work, and Pete was finished bagging and retrieving all the clothing and evidence, I stopped him.

"Pete, do you think you could do me a favor?"

"Anything you need."

"Would you mind sending me a copy of the photos, especially of the neck and face? I'd also like to have a copy of any evidence forms from the lab. I need some cases in which the evidence plays a big part, and this one might be a good one to use for teaching." I really didn't need the photographs, but I did need the lab evidence sheet for the hair. I had asked for photos on at least two dozen cases within the last 10 years, so the request wasn't at all unusual. However, the request for the lab forms was a first. I hoped asking for the two together wouldn't raise any eyebrows. Pete didn't ask.

Within a few days, I received both the photos and copies of the evidence sheets, including the chain of custody forms recording the hair taken from the body.

Now it was time to confront Brower. With fingers crossed, I called him on the phone. My previous muscle-bound guide answered the phone, for his gruff monotone was unmistakable.

"Dr. Jamison, Mr. Brower has no reason to speak with you any further." It was obvious the man knew all about my business arrangements with his boss.

"This is a call he'd better take," I asserted.

"And why is that?" He wasn't intimidated by my feeble threat. I needed to take another tact to get his attention.

"If he doesn't want to go to jail, he'd better take the call." That worked. Within minutes, Brower was on the line.

"What do you want?" Brower answered harshly. This was the first time I had heard him irritated. Gone was his soft-spoken demeanor.

"I think you'd better listen to me." I hoped the sound of my voice didn't duplicate the quivering I felt inside. This man made me feel uneasy just talking to him. Whenever we spoke, I felt like my life was on the brink of disaster. But now was not the time to lapse into a mass of cowardice; I had to sound convincing.

"Make this brief. I'm busy."

"I'll get right to the point. I have the means to make your life miserable."

"What the hell are you talking about?" He sounded more than irritated now.

"I'm guessing you won't want to hear the scientific basis for the certainty of DNA testing."

"Get to it!" he interrupted.

"We recently completed the autopsy of a young woman discovered near the building you own, the Franklin Building. She had been strangled. You might be interested to know that some of your hair was discovered on her body."

"First of all, I don't know anything about any dead woman and second of all, how do you know it's my hair?"

"I know it's your hair because I put it there." I let that sink in for a few seconds. "And you probably remember when and where I obtained it."

"So where are the cops? If it's my hair, why haven't I been arrested?"

"The DNA tests haven't been completed. And they won't be until I order it."

There was a short pause and then, "If I remember correctly, that hair has to be compared to something. What are the police going to use for a comparison?"

Brower surprised me with his intelligence. He knew enough to realize a sample from his body would be needed to compare to the evidence.

"I don't think it would be too difficult to convince the police to view you as a possible suspect and bring you in for questioning. I know a judge or two who might grant a warrant for you to submit a sample for comparison. Besides, the girl's body was discovered near the Franklin Building." I hoped this last little piece of information would help him understand the seriousness of my threat. It didn't.

"This is all bullshit. I doubt if my hair was really found on the body. You're trying my patience. What you're doing is not healthy."

"Do you have a fax number?" My question caught him off guard.

"Sure, why?"

"Give me the number, and I'll send you the proof. Think about what you read, and then you can let me know what you decide. One more thing. I've left letters of our dealings in safe places, just in case you get any ideas of harming Mary, her son, or me." I was beginning to feel the power of my words.

"Her son?" he questioned.

"Yes, her son. I'll expect your answer tomorrow."

I hung up the phone and faxed a copy of the evidence receipts from the lab. The paper contained all of the evidence submitted from the prostitute's autopsy, including the hair samples. I thought of how I would hate to be an employee in his house right now. I was sure the bodyguard who let me into the bathroom was probably in serious trouble. At least I hoped he was.

My main concern was the extent of Brower's influence. There was always the possibility he might have a judge or the prosecutor in his pocket. It would be difficult enough in the best of circumstances to convince the prosecutor to require Brower to give up blood or hair samples.

HIS ANSWER ARRIVED the first thing in the morning. I was seated at my desk when Shirley came in with a telegram.

"This is for you."

"What does it say?" I had always trusted her to open my mail for me.

"I didn't open it. You don't get very many of these, and I thought it might be personal."

I tore open the envelope and was taken aback by the two ominous words: *Show me!* I had just received my answer. My bluff had been called. Brower wasn't going to go away without a fight.

Shirley, sensing my reaction, asked if it were bad news. I quickly made up a story that someone I knew had just died.

"Oh, that's too bad. Who was it?"

"An old pathologist friend who lived in New York. He'd been sick for a while. You wouldn't know him."

"Do you plan to go to the funeral?"

"I don't know. I'll call later." My response was brusque, ending the conversation.

"I'm sorry," Shirley said as she backed out of my office.

Now that Brower had thrown down the gauntlet, the ball was in my court. My main problem was I didn't know what to do next. I would be hard pressed to go after a judge or the prosecutor so early in the investigation of the girl's death. I needed to figure out a way to intimidate Brower. But the only thing that he would probably respond to was force, and I certainly wasn't very forceful.

I'd been naïve to think the man would roll over because of a lab test. He would only become concerned if the results of a test pointed directly at him. I could imagine him ensconced behind his big polished desk, inwardly laughing at me. What a joke. Obviously I had to fight Brower with the same threat of force he was using on me. What I needed was someone who could confront him on his own turf. Who did I know that was tough enough to do it?

There were many big men in both the sheriff's office and the police department who were physically capable of doing the job. In addition to Deputy Hodin, there was Sgt. Arnie Jones who had also played some college football. He wasn't as large as Hodin, but he was just as intimidating. At six feet two inches and roughly 230 pounds, he had almost no body fat and was as strong as an ox. I'd love to see either one of these deputies square off against Brower's bodyguard.

But this was all wishful thinking. How could I get them or anyone else I knew to help without having to reveal too much information? I needed someone reliable who had the experience to be formidable but was also totally loyal to me. I was overlooking the obvious. Gus wasn't that big or young anymore, but he had that hardened, tough guy demeanor for the job. Would he be willing to help? I didn't know, but I had to take the chance. There was no one else. I'd ask him tomorrow.

THE NEXT MORNING I stopped by Dixie Donuts on the way to work and picked up a dozen glazed, powdered, chocolate-covered, and jelly-filled doughnuts. I found Gus making coffee in the downstairs lounge. He turned as I came through the doorway, and I tossed him the bag. He deftly caught it.

"Still have the fast reflexes," I complimented him.

"Not as good as they should be. In my prime, I would have heard you long before you threw the bag." He peeked inside. "Hmm. What are these for?"

"Thought you might like a little breakfast. I need to talk to you about something."

"The coffee's just about finished. Have a seat."

He poured me a cup in one of his extra mugs, a gift from a local funeral home.

"Where's your bagel?" he asked.

"I got these instead."

"This must be serious then." He knew I rarely changed my morning bagel routine.

Enough of the small talk. I needed his help, and I had to know if he would go out on a limb for me. My approach had to be direct and sound truthful. He'd know if he were being bullshitted.

"Gus, do you remember when I asked about Brower?"

"Sure."

"Well, I wasn't being very honest with you. He's a problem, and I need your help."

His initial response was to grab a powdered doughnut from the bag, dunk it in his coffee, and devour it in three bites. After finishing his second doughnut in similar fashion, he pulled a cigar from his pocket and unwrapped it. He clenched the side of his mouth around it. He didn't clip the end like the traditional cigar aficionados do. I guessed that was because he wasn't going to smoke it. When he finished this ritual, he was finally ready to listen.

"Go ahead."

I told him that Brower was pressuring Mrs. Thomas about some money her dead husband still owed him. I informed Gus that he'd become nasty and had even threatened to cause problems with her son who had some serious gambling debts.

"Why did she come to you and not the police?"

"He told her not to, and she's legitimately scared. She didn't know who else to turn to."

"And what can I do to help?"

"I was wondering if you could talk to Brower."

"Have you talked to him?"

"Me? No. To be honest, I don't think I'd be too successful dealing with a guy like that." Damn! I hated lying to this man.

"So let's say I go and rattle this guy's cage. What kind of leverage could I use? Why would he have to listen to me, a death investigator?"

"I've given that some thought."

"Go on."

"You could talk to him about the dead girl that we autopsied the other day who was found behind his building. Ask him about the girl, maybe even suggest that he's being considered seriously for involvement in her death because of the location of the body. Maybe you could mention there had been threats made to Mary, and you know he had dealings with her husband." My plan was really weak, and Gus recognized the holes very quickly. I think he also picked up on the fact that I had said Mary instead of Mrs. Thomas.

"Tell me about you and Mrs. Thomas."

"I used to be in love with her or should I say, I thought I was. We lived together in college for a short time before she sent me packing."

"Used to be in love with her?" He stared at me. It was obvious to him that Mary was still an important part of my life, and I was a lousy liar.

"Oh, I don't know. Maybe I still do. I'm trying not to think about her. I had almost forgotten about my feelings for her after all these years, and then her husband died and she drifted into my life again." For the first time during the conversation, I was being truthful.

Seemingly lost in thought, Gus absently twirled the cigar in his mouth. Finally he looked up and said he needed time to think about my request.

"I'll get back to you soon."

"I appreciate it, Gus."

THIS WAS ALL SO DRAINING. I was exhausted. All the lying, repressing my feelings for Mary, planning my revenge against Brower, losing my dog, was too much. The situation was sapping my mental and emotional strength. A part of me wanted to run away from it all and not deal with it any more, but my practical side told me this wouldn't work because I would be leaving Mary to the mercy of a well-dressed hooligan. My last chance was Gus. I hoped he'd come through for me.

26

Karen was on call, but she had only one case. A chronic, drug-abusing alcoholic had been found dead in a local motel room. The man had been passing through Springfield from Oklahoma on his way to St. Louis.

I watched Karen work. The dead man's liver was shrunken and scarred. She knew this cirrhotic condition was seen in less than 20 percent of alcoholics. The knobby liver surface could also be caused by hepatitis, a common complication of drug abusers. She talked aloud to me as if I were a student, reminding me that the distinction between alcoholism or drug abuse as a cause of the failed liver didn't matter because his death was still due to natural causes.

Her only concern was whether or not he might have died of an overdose due to alcohol, drugs, or both. If that were the case, then his death would be ruled an accident. To be complete, Karen ordered a drug screen to make sure his system wasn't filled with some noxious substance.

"Mark, have you heard anything more from the commissioners?" Karen was still concerned about her future.

"I spoke to Stanley Garland the other day. He was still giving me the party line about how the other commissioners were worried about our projected costs compared to last year."

"What did you tell him?"

"I told him if he didn't like the way I ran this office, he could find someone else for the job."

My forthrightness startled her. "Oh," was her only response. She was in the process of cutting open the man's heart when I gave her the news, but she didn't miss a knife stroke. I wondered if she was now thinking that she might not only get to keep her job, but she might actually have a chance to run the show if I left. Little did she know the budget might not be the only reason she could become the new chief.

Before I went home for the evening, Gus stopped by my office.

"Doc, may I sit?"

I waved him down into the chair in front of me. He sat down and quickly gave me the answer I desperately needed.

"I think I can help you out. But you have to agree to do it my way."

"Whatever you think. You're doing me the favor."

"I'm asking Sid to come with me. I've already asked him, and he's agreed. I know you probably didn't want him to know anything about this, but I need him."

"Why?" I was perturbed that he'd talked to someone else without asking me first.

"Sid will give the meeting more credibility. Brower will understand if it's a policeman investigating a homicide. Sid can ask about the dead woman while I finish letting Brower know how I feel about his bothering Mrs. Thomas and her son. You know that Sid and I are close friends. He's not one to talk about things. He's aware of what kind of guy Brower is, and he admitted that he'd enjoy making him feel the pinch. Besides, we're not doing anything illegal. If anyone complains, he has a legitimate reason to be investigating the girl's death."

I had to trust Gus on this one. What choice did I have anyway? He might be saving my butt, literally. I had asked for his help, and it wasn't up to me to question his methods.

"When do you plan to talk to Brower?"

"The sooner the better. We'll try to make a little visit in the morning."

I DIDN'T SLEEP MUCH that night. Sleuth was in heaven, at least she was the first two times I took her for a walk. It was a different story when I attempted to take her out about 3:30 A.M. for the fourth time. She rebelled. I couldn't even drag her out the bedroom door. I went without her for another half-hour walk, and then I was finally able to sleep for a couple of hours. Another weary day lay ahead.

GUS CAME TO FIND ME an hour before noon.

"You're back already?"

"It didn't take long. We only talked to him for about 20 minutes."

"What did he say?"

"Not much. He's a cool one. He didn't show any visible

signs of distress. In fact, he didn't even raise his voice. He simply said he wasn't involved, and it would be impossible for anyone to connect him to the crime. Sid pressured him, and his feathers weren't even ruffled."

"What about Mrs. Thomas?"

"When Sid was finished, I asked Brower if he knew her. He said he did, but hadn't seen her in a while. I told him that was a lie, and it had come to my attention he'd been bothering her."

"Did he respond?"

"Not really. He just sat there behind that big desk of his and played dumb. The man's dirty, I can tell. Be hard to prove, though. He did say something I found strange."

"What was that?"

"He said to tell you he didn't appreciate you sending me."

"Why do you think he said that?" I asked.

"Beats me. Have you spoken to him?"

"Well, no. Mary must have admitted that she'd talked to me." I didn't know if my lie sounded credible or not.

Gus looked at me and seemed to accept my explanation. I quickly changed the subject.

"Do you think he got the message?"

"Can't say. He didn't look like he'd even consider taking orders. It's my guess he's used to giving them. I doubt he got that fancy house and all those expensive cars by doing things by the book. He's also got a couple of hard cases working for him. Sid recognized one of his boys who's well-known to the police."

"Gus, I appreciate your doing this for me. I owe you."

"No problem," he responded. "At first I didn't want to get

involved with this. I thought the police should handle it. But while I was talking to the guy and watching his bodyguards, I almost wished they had tried something. I don't like his kind or his friends. They're up to no good. Probably have good lawyers to keep them looking respectable."

"Thanks again," I repeated.

"Sure thing. Let me know if he bothers you or Mrs. Thomas again." He headed for the door.

The phone rang as soon as Gus left my office.

"Doctor, Mr. Brower is calling. Do you want to take it?"

Damn, that was quick! I was glad Gus had left when the call came through since I told him I hadn't spoken with Brower. I didn't want him to catch me in another lie.

"Doctor, we need to talk." Brower's voice was even and he didn't seem angry, probably a good sign. Maybe we could reach some kind of a compromise.

"When?"

"Can you meet this evening, say about eight?"

"I can do that. Where?"

AS I DROVE TO MEET BROWER, my spirits were high. I had to believe that this entire affair was finally coming to a conclusion. Gus and Sid's involvement was exactly what I'd needed to force Brower into negotiating. I doubted I could get away cleanly from all this, but I thought I might escape with a little bit of luck.

Now that the sun was setting, there were few people and little traffic on the streets. I pulled into the alley behind the Franklin Building, a convenient location for Brower since he had an office on the top floor. He'd probably been working late. There was a delivery door at the back of the building. I parked my car across the alley from the door just as Brower had suggested and waited. A few minutes later the door opened and two men emerged.

The larger man was easy to distinguish. Brower, no small man at just over six feet, appeared scrawny next to his bodyguard, the one I recognized from his house. I exited from my car and stood next to the open door. It was a short distance from the delivery door to my car, but Mr. Muscles and Brower disregarded me as they stopped to look up and down the alley. Clearly satisfied that we were alone, the two men approached me with the hulk in the lead.

I wasn't surprised as I watched the big man's hands reach behind his back and produce a gun. I instantly realized the last thing on their minds was talk. Without conscious thought, I dropped down behind my car door to grab my gun from under the front seat, and as I did so, he fired. My sudden movement caused him to miss. I recognized the shock on his face as I stood up and pulled the trigger of my gun. I thought I'd hit him, but he didn't fall or stagger. I pointed my gun at his chest, exactly as Gus had taught me, and fired a second time. Just as I squeezed the trigger, his second shot hit me, throwing me backwards against the frame of the car.

27

Gus had listened to my entire story in the hospital without comment. He was silent even when he discovered I'd lied to him. Somehow I knew he understood why I couldn't tell him what was happening. He always seemed to know how I felt. I was ashamed that I'd lied to him, almost as ashamed as I felt for falsifying the Thomas death certificate. His only visible response was to sit back in his chair and swirl his cigar in his mouth

"Gus."

"Yes."

"How did you know I needed help? You must have followed me."

"I did," he answered quietly.

"But how did you know?"

He explained that I hadn't been my normal self for the past few weeks. He knew something was wrong, but he didn't know what. My sense of urgency in learning how to shoot was somewhat suspicious. But what really tipped him off was when I had lied to him about knowing Brower. He'd heard Shirley tell me that Brower was on the line and then stood outside my door, listening to the conversation.

"So you eavesdropped?"

"Yes," he admitted unabashedly.

"Well, I'm glad you did."

Gus relaxed after hearing me say those words.

"Gus, there's one thing I can't figure out."

"What's that?"

"Just before he fired at me, Brower said, 'You're not going to pin his death on me.' He said *his* and not *her*. I don't think he was referring to the prostitute."

"Maybe he wasn't thinking right. He was about to kill you. Maybe the stress of the situation caused him to use the wrong word," Gus guessed.

"Probably, but he didn't seem all that stressed to me. He seemed to be taking care of business. Another day on the job," I said sarcastically.

Gus didn't respond.

"Gus, is everything okay about your role in this fiasco? Is the department convinced that killing Brower was the only option you had?"

"There's no problem, Doc. Sid questioned me after the shooting. He told me not to worry."

I felt reassured that nothing was going to happen to Gus as the result of my stupidity.

"Gus, I'm tired. I need to get some rest. Don't you have some work to do?"

"You get some sleep. I'll go get something to eat." He was leaving as the nurse came in to give me another shot for the pain.

"This Demerol is pretty good stuff," I said to myself with a grin.

I AWOKE IN THE NIGHT. The usual hospital noises surrounded me. The pain in my shoulder was subsiding; now it was just a dull ache. Feeling stronger, I attempted to get out of bed. I swung my legs over the side and touched my feet to the cool linoleum floor. The IV in my arm presented a problem until I figured out how to negotiate the pole carrying the bag of fluid. I took a tentative step and felt lightheaded. The chair Gus usually sat in was only a few feet away, so I shuffled in that direction and sat down, breathing heavily from the effort. I decided to sit for a while before I made the trek back to bed.

With nothing else to do in the semidarkness, I began to think. Brower's words stuck in my mind: *You're not going to pin his death on me.* Who was he referring to? I could understand if someone was so afraid, he might make a slip in using the wrong word, but this man didn't seem nervous or agitated in the least. It just didn't make any sense. The only deaths he could possibly be interested in were the prostitute, the camper's wife, and John Thomas. Thomas was the only man of the three, and he certainly wasn't murdered.

New ideas kept clouding my mind. Could he have had something to do with the death of Mary's husband? I didn't see how. I went over all of the facts concerning Thomas's death. The man had left home, presumably for work. The circumstances and the times had been checked out—there was nothing in the autopsy that suggested foul play—the drug screen had been negative—Thomas had serious heart disease—the scene was unremarkable—the car had run into the bridge—the man was obviously dead or dying by the time he'd hit the bridge....

Was there anything suspicious about the car? I certainly didn't remember anything out of order. I thought I'd looked in the front seat. Had I looked in the back seat? I couldn't remember. I needed some more sleep. Maybe I was becoming paranoid about conspiracies. The few steps back to the bed were slightly easier than my maiden voyage. I lay down exhausted from the effort and slept until morning.

GUS WAS SITTING IN THE CHAIR, munching on a doughnut when I woke up. There were crumbs and a snowstorm of powdered sugar dusting his blue-striped tie. His coffee was on the floor. He was just bending down to pick up the paper cup when he realized I was watching him.

"Good morning," he said. "How's the shoulder?"

"Not bad. It throbs some."

"I think you're going to make it," Gus smiled.

"Gus, Brower's remark is still bothering me. I was thinking about it last night. Do you think he could have been referring to Dr. Thomas's death?"

"But he wasn't murdered, Doc. Didn't the man have a bad heart?"

"Yes, he had heart disease. Could I have missed something?

There wasn't anything unusual about the autopsy. That only leaves the scene."

"Do you want me to check it out?" Gus volunteered.

"I'd appreciate that. Sgt. Patterson worked the scene. Maybe you could talk to him. I remember looking inside the car, but maybe I overlooked something there. Patterson likes to take photographs of good accidents. Maybe he took some inside the car."

Gus said he'd get right on it. He seemed pleased to have something to do instead of sitting around watching me recuperate. Before he left, he alerted me that Sid was busy this morning, but he'd be coming by to question me later in the afternoon. Gus said he wanted to be with me when I talked to Sid.

Well-wishers began arriving soon after Gus's departure. Shirley was first, intent on mothering me for a while. She observed the nurses performing their duties and gave her silent approval or disapproval as she evaluated the quality of care I was receiving. Bill and Karen visited in the early afternoon. Bill brought me a magazine with stories about the Old West. Karen assured me all was well at the office. She ran a couple of cases by me to see if I was interested. I didn't have any suggestions to offer.

I still hadn't heard from Mary. I was surprised she hadn't called or visited.

Gus came back about 2:00. He was carrying a folder of photos from the Thomas crash site. He handed the folder to me before sitting down.

"Can't see much from these," Gus said, "Oh, I almost forgot. Sgt. Patterson sends his regards."

DEADLY DECEIT

I sifted through the file of pictures. Most of them were of the scene, showing damage to the car and bridge. There were only five photos of the car's interior. One focused on the back seat area and four dealt with the front. Three of the front seat shots showed the collapsed airbag, and the body and its position. The other showed the passenger's side, including the floor. There were papers littering both the seat and the floor as well as what looked like a broken ceramic coffee mug.

The photographs stimulated my memory. I remembered the papers and a coffee cup. I didn't remember the type of cup, but I did remember the cup.

"You're right, Gus. There isn't much here."

"If you think Brower meant Thomas in his remark, then Brower must know something we don't know. But how could he have information that someone caused the man's death?" Gus was talking more to himself than to me.

"It's impossible, Gus. There was absolutely no evidence that Thomas was murdered. How could Brower know more than we do based on all the evidence we put together from the scene and the autopsy?" Now I was talking more to myself.

"You already know the answer to that, Doc. He couldn't know anything, unless it was something that would never show up in a regular autopsy."

"So you tell me, Gus, what could kill a person that doesn't show up in an regular autopsy?"

"Well, based on all you've taught me, the possibilities are fairly limited. He could have been suffocated, but that's not likely since witnesses confirmed he was driving alone prior to the accident. I guess there could have been blunt trauma to the head with no external signs, but you'd have picked something up when you did the internal autopsy. He had to have died from natural causes, and you found definite evidence of heart disease. There's no way this could have been a murder."

My mind was racing. "You're forgetting poison, Gus. Poison can go undetected and still cause a person to die."

"But Doc, you did a drug screen and there was no evidence of any poison."

"Gus, we did the standard screen which tests for drugs of abuse. We never thought about ordering a screen for poison."

"That seems so farfetched. What kind of poison can be timed so that the victim is sure to be driving when the effects finally take hold, making it look like an accidental death? What poisonous substance releases itself into the blood at a specific time? There's just no way." Gus seemed utterly bewildered by these new possibilities.

"The poison would have to be administered in a form that dissolves while . . . while. . . . "

Our minds clicked in unison.

"While drinking his coffee," we both concluded.

"You know what you're suggesting?" Gus asked.

"I know exactly what I'm suggesting, Gus. Thomas was drinking coffee on his way to work. It was probably a regular routine, just like my bagel habit and your doughnut routine. If someone wanted to kill Thomas and have it look like an accident, all they'd have to know is that he always drank his coffee on the way to work. If the murderer could gain access to that coffee before Thomas carried it to its car, the poison could work its magic while the doctor was driving. He would die on the way to work, and everyone would naturally assume he died from the accident."

DEADLY DECEIT

"Let me get this straight, Doc. Let's say someone put a poisonous substance in Thomas's coffee, a substance that was known to work quickly enough to affect the doctor on his way to...." Gus abruptly stopped thinking aloud when a nurse entered the room to take my vital signs and ask how I was doing.

While she was in the room, I kept pondering the possibilities of this unique scenario. If the coffee was the method of introducing poison into the man's system, then someone in the Thomas house was the culprit. It was a staggering thought.

As soon as the nurse finished her requisite duties, I vented to my friend.

"Gus, I don't know if I can handle where all this speculation is going. If someone poisoned the doctor's coffee, it had to be someone close to him. It had to be someone who knew his coffee-drinking habits, and someone who had access to his cup before he carried it to his car."

"I hear you, Doc. I was thinking the same thing. Once again, the possibilities are limited. Do you know who was at the house when you went to tell Mrs. Thomas about her husband's death?"

"Only Mary and her son that I know of. I'm sure they have a cook, but I don't remember if she was there."

I didn't know what to do next. The thought of anyone killing Dr. Thomas seemed like such a remote possibility. All my suspicions were based on one small word uttered by a man who was in the process of shooting me. I just couldn't believe Mary or her son would be capable of murder.

"What do you want me to do?" Gus brought me back to reality.

"I don't know, Gus. What do you think?"

He looked at me with surprise. I was usually the one who formulated the plan, not the other way around.

"Your hunch is kind of weak, but it would be easy to follow up. All we have to do is test his blood for any substances that might not have come up in the regular tox screen."

He was right. It wouldn't be difficult for the toxicologist to recheck the blood. But there were hundreds of poisons that could kill someone. The toxicologist would need some kind of focus because he couldn't run tests for all poisonous compounds in the universe.

"Let's start from the beginning. In any case of a suspected overdose, we would contact the family to see if the victim was taking any regular medicines. Then we'd talk to the family physician and double check. Right?" Gus was giving me a lesson in Investigation 101.

"I know Mary was worried about her husband's chest pain, but she said he refused to go to the doctor."

Gus only frowned at my answer before stating the obvious. "And if she were involved in his death, she'd tell you the truth?"

This question stunned me. Mary would never lie to me. But I'd been wrong before, so I couldn't let this suspicion go unproven.

"All right. Maybe you can talk to some of his colleagues and see if he'd been seeing a physician. Meanwhile, I'll alert the toxicologist. Maybe we should keep this investigation under wraps until we find out if there's anything to go on."

"That sounds like a plan I can live with. Now, one more thing. Sid is going to be here in less than 30 minutes. He needs to ask some questions. I've already talked to him about how you were approached by Mr. Brower to help cover up the camper wife's death. He knows that you told Brower to go to hell and Brower came after you because you wouldn't break the law. Do you have the story straight?" He wasn't asking as much as telling me what to say to Sid.

28

Gus was saving my butt again. This story would sound plausible and keep the real story quiet for the time being. There might be some more media coverage. Actually there had already been two days of front-page news, but no reasons for the shooting had been given to date.

Sid was right on time. After spending less than 20 minutes with me, he seemed satisfied with the story Gus had instructed me to give. Sid indicated that the investigation would still be pending for a while, but the news should die down within a couple of days.

Around 4:30, I called the toxicologist. He was based at St. Mary's Hospital and we had worked together for the last 13 years. Herb Tolbert was as good as any academic toxicologist

I had ever met. He had published numerous articles, many of which were about forensic cases I had sent his way. The lab, almost nonexistent when he was first hired by the hospital, had gained a quality reputation under his guidance and expertise.

"Herb, this is Mark."

"Mark, good to hear from you. I'm sorry I haven't been in to see you. How are you making out?"

"As good as expected for a one-armed pathologist," I joked.

"One-armed? I thought you were okay. Did you lose the use of your arm?" he said with concern. Herb never was able to understand my morbid sense of humor.

"No, Herb, I was just kidding. I'm fine."

"Oh, good. What can I do for you?"

"I need some help on a case. I need to know more about poisons. What substance could be used in coffee to cause someone's death?"

Herb relished the opportunity to do a little teaching. "Oh, there are any number of substances that can do the job, but most of them taste bad, and they have to be used in large quantities. The victims get sick, but they usually don't die. Some eventually die, but they linger for a while. Repeat exposures are the most effective."

"Herb, it's got to be a substance that would be undetected and would cause death in, oh, maybe 15 to 20 minutes."

"Well, why didn't you say so? The most common poisons that have been used with any frequency to kill people suddenly are strychnine and cyanide. Of course, the strychnine is kind of bitter. The taste would have to be masked with some cream or sugar."

"Okay, that's what I need to know. I'd like you to pull a case I did recently and check it for those two substances."

"Sure thing. Do you know the case number?"

"I don't have it with me, but I'll have Gus call it in later."

"Fine. I'll get right on it when I get the number. And Mark, I'm glad to hear you're doing so well."

"Thanks, Herb."

GUS CAME BY AROUND DINNERTIME. He took one look at the hospital food on my lap table and turned up his nose. I didn't think the meatloaf, potatoes and green beans were so bad. It had been a couple of days since I'd had a full meal, so I would have eaten anything remotely edible. He did bring me a Louis L'Amour book of short stories I hadn't read.

I briefed Gus about my conversation with Herb. Gus had already checked out Dr. Thomas's medical history with some of the doctor's colleagues and was prepared to bring me up to date.

"You know, I don't like talking to physicians. Most of them are so tightassed, it's like pulling teeth. They think they're giving away state secrets if they talk about one of their own, especially if it's one of their friends. Nothing personal, Doc."

I held my grin in check. "I understand. What did you find out?"

"The man did complain of some indigestion over the past few years. One of his partners thought he might have had some heart disease, but he didn't know for sure. He gave me the name of a cardiologist friend, a Dr. Martin, but he wasn't in today. I'll try to contact him tomorrow."

"Well, it doesn't look like there's much there. Let me know after you talk to Dr. Martin."

Gus couldn't stay long. No one else dropped by, so I drifted in and out of sleep watching some television and reading a few of the short stories Gus had brought me.

The surgeon, an infrequent visitor, dropped by late in the evening. He examined my dressing, asked me a few perfunctory questions, and quickly shot out of the room. He obviously had more important patients to deal with. His bedside manner didn't impress me much, but then I didn't particularly care if it was good or not. He had an excellent reputation as a surgeon, and that's what was most important. He did tell me to take a couple of trips up and down the hall to get some exercise, because he didn't want me to develop blood clots in my legs from inactivity. I planned to do as he said. I'd had too many cases over the years of people dying from blood clots that had developed in their legs after surgery. The clots would break loose and travel up through the heart and plug up the major blood vessels leading to the lungs. Death tended to be sudden. I committed myself to be a model patient.

Later that evening, the head nurse informed me that I could go home the next morning if I promised to take it easy. Attempting a little humor, I told her I didn't think that was possible because I was training to run a marathon. My attempt at levity didn't register. She just admonished me about getting the dressing wet.

THE NEXT MORNING, GUS CALLED. I gave him the good news about my discharge. He congratulated me and then shared his news. He'd spoken with Dr. Martin. Dr. Thomas had started seeing him over a year ago for some chest pain, and Dr. Martin had prescribed nitroglycerin for the occasional discomfort. Dr. Thomas was scheduled for some studies on his heart the month after he died to check on the progression of his disease. His EKG revealed he had suffered a minor heart attack sometime in the past. I was surprised that Mary didn't know about this.

"Why didn't he get it treated sooner?" Gus asked.

"Doctors are some of the worst patients. I don't think they want to believe they're vulnerable to disease like everyone else. That's common in the medical profession."

"Pretty stupid if you ask me."

"I agree. Gus, I need you to call Herb and give him the Thomas case number. He's going to run some more thorough testing."

"Be glad to. Will too much nitroglycerin cause a sudden death?" he asked.

"Sure. Too much of any medicine can kill you. Have Herb check for nitro too."

Within the next hour I was unhooked from my IV, given a cursory exam and my walking papers, and sent home. Karen came by to offer me a ride. We discussed what had transpired at work in the last 24 hours.

Relishing her role as my guardian, Karen helped me from the car when we arrived home. I was surprised by her compassionate behavior. The first noise I heard was Sleuth's insistent barking, and I was momentarily saddened at the thought that Mort wouldn't be part of my homecoming. I still missed him. We went in the front door, but Sleuth didn't jump on me with her usual vigor. I must have smelled very strange and medicinal to her, so she was a little bit cautious. I bent down and stroked her head until she loosened up.

Still weak, I made my way directly to the couch. The simple task of coming home was more taxing than I'd ever thought it could be. Karen made sure I was comfortable and shifted a few sofa pillows around my back before heading back to work. Except for the dog, who had now jumped onto the couch next to me, the house seemed unbearably quiet. I instinctively grabbed the remote control and turned on the television. For the next hour, I surfed back and forth through the channels. Little was on that held my interest. I couldn't get Mary out of my mind. The thought of her being involved in her husband's death was unbelievable. I had to be patient. The toxicology tests would prove that I was being overly mistrustful.

The IV fluids I'd been given during my hospitalization were now running through my system with a vengeance, and I had to make constant trips to the bathroom. In between visits, I looked through the stacks of letters and bills neatly piled on the kitchen table. Gus had efficiently taken care of the mail, papers, and Sleuth while I was recuperating.

Gus interrupted my boredom. He knocked on the front door shortly after noon. I yelled for him to come in, but Karen had locked the door on her way out. I slowly rose and ambled across the room. My speed wasn't very impressive.

"Gus, good to see you. I just finished going through the mail. Thanks for bringing it in." Sleuth approached Gus, and he took time out to scratch behind her ears.

"No problem. Let's sit."

I didn't know if he made the suggestion because I looked

like I was about to keel over or because he wanted to break some bad news to me. It turned out to be the latter.

"Mark, Herb called me about half an hour ago. He said he didn't have to run the test for nitroglycerin because he'd already found something."

"What did he find?" I really didn't want to hear the answer.

"Cyanide."

"Damn. How much?"

"Enough that Dr. Thomas's death was no accident."

My anguish must have been apparent. Gus gave me time to deal with the news. I found it almost impossible to meet his gaze.

"Mark."

"Yes," I answered mechanically.

"We have to take this to the police. I know how difficult this must be for you, but it has to be taken to the authorities."

"I guess so. Gus, none of this makes sense."

"I know. I'm going to call Sid. Mark, we have to tell him all of it."

"You're right." My response was weak. Gus rose and left to make the call.

I had remained in decent control with all that had happened before now. But the realization that Mary might have been involved in killing her husband put me over the edge. I sat paralyzed in the chair.

Gus returned and said he'd called Sid, who would be over in about an hour.

We passed the time waiting in total silence.

Sid joined us around the kitchen table. I didn't even attempt to pretend that the toxicology test proving cyanide was anything but totally devastating. Somehow I summoned up a reserve of courage and began my confession. It took me more than 30 minutes to tell Sid the whole story. He interrupted me only a few times with questions.

"This could get pretty messy," Sid said, without making any value judgments. Of course, he had every right to be critical. Throughout his career he'd seen plenty of good people fall prey to bad judgment because of drugs, money, love, or sex. My story wasn't anything new. He studied my face with compassion. We had been associates and friends, although not close personal ones, for many years.

"I'm not sure how all this is going to go down. I'll do what I can to help." His sincerity was heartfelt.

"You know you can count on us," Gus added.

"One more thing," Sid stated.

"What's that?"

"I think it would be a good idea for you to turn everything having to do with these cases over to your assistant."

"I'll take care of that immediately."

They quietly left me to deal with the consequences of my own flawed behavior.

29

Karen came over as soon as she finished her cases for the afternoon. I'd asked her to stop by because I needed to tell her the same story I'd shared with Sid. I owed her the truth, in my own words, from my own lips. The hours I spent waiting for her were interminable. I couldn't stop chastising myself for my own stupidity, and I felt incredibly embarrassed to admit my failings to a colleague. I guess my ego was still fragile.

I shuffled to the door to answer her knock. She was dressed smartly in a business suit, looking every bit the part of the chief medical examiner she was soon to become.

"Hi. Feeling better?" she inquired.

"Like a million. Don't I look it?"

Karen smiled faintly. She never seemed to appreciate my feeble attempts at being cute.

"Okay, so I don't look too great. At least you could try lying to me," I grinned. I didn't receive a reciprocal smile.

I led Karen into the kitchen, and asked her if she wanted some coffee.

"No, thanks, Mark. I can't stay long. My parents and I are going out to dinner."

I wondered what the occasion was. She was clearly all business today. "Please sit down, Karen. What I have to tell you may take some time. And I need to get it all off my chest before I chicken out," I said seriously.

Karen studied my face, obviously trying to gauge my sincerity level, and then extracted her cell phone from her purse. Without any initial pleasantries, she instructed her parents to go to dinner without her because something important had come up at the office. She replaced her phone in her purse and said she'd take me up on the proffered cup of coffee.

I poured two cups and placed them on the table.

"Do you have any milk and sweetener, Mark? Just head me in the right direction—you've clearly had a tough day."

It was the first hint of kindness in her demeanor, so I let her feel useful while I tried to collect my thoughts. She was oddly at home in my bachelor kitchen, retrieving the milk from the refrigerator and the sugar from the cupboard without any prodding. I found it strange that I didn't know what she took in her coffee even though we'd worked together for more than a year. I guess you never know someone as well as you think you do, as she'd soon discover when I was done telling my story.

"It's easiest if you just start at the beginning, Mark."

"I know, Karen. I'm just struggling to find the right words. If you wouldn't mind, I'd like to give you the entire story before you ask me any questions. That'll be easier for me."

"Whatever works for you, Mark. Go ahead."

I spent the next hour, interrupted by another cup of coffee and several trips to the bathroom, going over everything that had happened from the time I returned from the San Diego conference to the present. I didn't omit anything except for some of the more intimate details of my relationship with Mary. Karen winced a few times, especially when I told her about Mort. When I confessed I'd committed the fraudulent act of falsifying Dr. Thomas's death certificate, her eyes registered a pitiful combination of shock and disbelief. It was almost enough to make me freeze up, but I knew I had to finish the story right then, or I'd never be able to live with myself.

She seemed utterly dumbfounded when I reached the end. To avoid some silly expression of condolence, she escaped into the nuts and bolts of her job.

"When should I re-sign the Thomas death certificate?" She was eager to set things right.

"I think you should do it as quickly as possible. I don't know when the story is going to hit the papers, but you should be ready when it does. Maybe in the morning. Look at the Thomas file and then talk to Gus and Sid Freeman. You'll want to do it before the phone starts ringing."

"Any idea how much the media knows?"

"I don't know for sure. It depends on how Sid carries out the rest of the investigation within the police department."

Karen sat back in her chair, took a deep breath, and paused to think.

"Mark, I'm so sorry about all of this." Her look of compassion appeared genuine. "Is there anything I can do for you?"

"No. I appreciate your concern. But this is a mess I've gotten myself into, and I'll have to deal with the consequences."

"What's going to happen to you?"

"Hmm.... I guess I'm going to stay home here to recuperate and then I'll see what's in store for me. I doubt if I'll have my job much longer. That means you'll be the chief. At least you will if I have any say in the matter. But I doubt my recommendation will carry any weight with the commissioners. There's no question you're the best person for the job, and I believe you'll do quite well. You're a good forensic pathologist, Karen, and you deserve to be in charge."

Karen's eyes began to mist over, and she appeared truly touched. She rose, came around the table and gave me an awkward hug while I was still seated. I wasn't sure if she was giving me the hug because she felt sorry for me, or because her dreams of being chief had finally come true. In an effort to avoid being cynical, I decided it must be the former.

She left a few minutes later, and a wave of relief engulfed me. I needed to spend some time alone, licking my wounds. Rehashing the story again, this time for my successor, had depleted my sadly lacking supply of courage.

SLEEP THAT NIGHT WAS IMPOSSIBLE. I kept remembering what a fool I'd been, and when I finished beating myself up for that, I focused on how I'd ruined a fine career that had been years in the making. While I still held onto a flickering hope that Mary wasn't involved in the death of her husband, my more rational moments pointed me toward her complicity. My heart kept waiting for the phone to ring, with Mary assuring me that all the evidence would prove her innocence. Deeply entangled in this complicated morass of thoughts, I knew that even Louis L'Amour couldn't provide the escape I needed.

AS DAWN APPROACHED, I put on my robe, let Sleuth out into the backyard, and made a fresh pot of coffee. The pot was getting a good workout these days. I couldn't imagine surviving without loading up on caffeine each day. I opened the front door to retrieve the newspaper with trepidation, half expecting the media to be gathered in the front yard. But the yard and the street were singularly silent, allowing me a brief respite before the storm. The sun was rising, and I brightened to the new day. I tried to restrain my automatic feelings that maybe, somehow, everything might turn out all right. The newspaper was on the porch and I carried it back inside.

There was nothing in the headlines about Dr. Thomas's death. The main article featured a disastrous flood in Arkansas where hundreds of homes were on the verge of being destroyed. It seemed ironic that good old Mother Nature was still wrecking havoc on the land, when all signs seemed to indicate that man was doing enough on his own to cause disasters. I read the article with halfhearted interest, knowing I should feel fortunate that I still had a roof over my head. My thoughts were interrupted by the irritating ring of the phone.

"Mark, this is Mary."

I almost dropped the receiver, then quickly recovered, trying not to sound too anxious.

"Mary?"

"Mark, I have to talk to you." Her pleading voice was soft and sensuous, but also insistent.

I allowed my common sense to speak, instead of my somewhat battered heart.

"Mary, I don't think that's a very good idea."

"Why not? You don't really believe I could have had anything to do with John's death, do you?"

I didn't know how to respond. Did I believe she killed her husband? No, but I'd seen too many horrendous and totally unexpected crimes over the years. I knew my gut instincts could always be wrong.

"Mary, I don't think we should be talking. Have the police been in touch with you yet?"

"Of course they have. They came to the house last night and told me that John's death was due to cyanide poisoning in his coffee. I know that cyanide is a poison, but how would I know where to get it and how to use it in coffee? My circle of lady friends doesn't happen to include any women who have been plotting to kill their husbands." She continued to plead her case.

I expected Mary to be righteously indignant that she had been accused of murdering her husband. Instead she seemed hellbent on convincing me that the use of cyanide wasn't in her bag of tricks. While I felt better just hearing her voice no matter what she was saying, I knew we shouldn't be having this conversation. More than anything I wanted her to be standing on my doorstep, her period of mourning over, and her hopes pinned on the man who still loved her. But I realized I had to end it. I had to cut this conversation short if I had any hope of saving myself.

"Mary, I need to go. Maybe we'll be able to get together soon. Let's see what transpires in the next few days before we try to come to any conclusions."

There was silence on the end of the phone, then she said, "Mark, I do care for you," and before I could respond, the line went dead.

As quickly as that it was over. I felt empty and somehow used. Even a long, hot bath didn't help. By the time I'd dressed, Karen had called, needing a few more details about the Thomas autopsy and investigation. I answered her brief questions and she said she had to get back to work. It seemed as though it was business as usual at the medical examiner's office. I wasn't there and I felt estranged and alone. What had I done? I'd thrown away the key to the only place I'd ever really belonged.

THE FRUSTRATING PART was not knowing what was happening in the outside world. Before, I always knew, either from Gus or law enforcement, about each new piece of evidence in every case and investigation. Now I was a hermit, cut off from my friends, my colleagues, and the news. Then suddenly, as if I had telepathic powers directly connected to Gus, the phone rang. Thankfully, it was my friend.

"How are you doing, Doc?"

"I was just thinking about you, Gus."

"You were?"

"Yes. I was hoping you'd call sometime and give me an update."

"Well, your wish has been magically granted." His pathetic attempt to sound like a genie at least made me smile. "What do you wish to know, my master?"

"Have you heard anything about my job?"

He adopted a more serious tone. "No, but I expect you'll hear soon. If I were the commissioners, I'd put you on leave as quickly as possible. They need to distance themselves from you."

I was somewhat surprised to find Gus so insightful about the political arena. His intuition was usually right on target.

"I guess you're right. Is there anything new in the investigation?"

"There sure is. That's why I called."

"So give it to me." His speech seemed so measured and slow, I'd have throttled him if he'd been within striking distance. I was about to go crazy waiting for him to give me the latest information.

"Sid asked me to accompany him when he questioned Mrs. Thomas and her son. He wanted to talk to both, separately of course, but the boy wasn't home."

"Well, how did the conversation go? Did you learn anything new? Has her story changed?" I tried not to sound too hopeful.

"Mark, hang on. I'm getting to that."

"Sorry."

"She was the perfect lady. Sid asked about her involvement with you. She answered that she had briefly been involved with you, but it was a mistake, and it was definitely over. She indicated that she had no strong feelings for you, and was not interested in you in any way." Gus paused to let that tiny little bombshell sink in.

"Go on," I replied, ready now to ingest all of the bad news at once.

"Sid then pursued the Brower issue and asked her if she had any ideas about why you might have had cause to kill him. She professed total ignorance. Sid pressed her about her relationship with Brower and asked if the two of them were intimate. She acted shocked and said that was absurd."

"Do you think she was telling the truth?"

"Of course not. She was lying. She's smooth though, I have to give her that."

I wondered if maybe Gus and Sid were not reading Mary correctly. She had just sounded so sincere on the phone.

"What happened then?"

"Sid told her that her husband's death was no accident, but rather a clear case of premeditated murder. She acted astonished and then began to cry. She left the room to find a handkerchief. Not a bad performance, but then she made a mistake."

"What did she do?" Gus knew how to keep me in suspense.

"She asked, in-between sobs, 'Do you have any idea who would have wanted to poison him like that?'"

"Damn," I responded. How could she possibly have known about the poison if she hadn't been involved? I knew Sid couldn't have let it slip earlier. It was too much of a coincidence that she would bring up that cause of death from all of the other possible causes. Most people, on hearing the word "murder," naturally assume the death was caused by a gunshot wound or stabbing.

"Yeah, and then she saw me look at Sid, and she knew she'd said the wrong thing. After that she refused to say another word, and the questioning was over. She got up and led us to the door. She did thank us for the information and acted like the stricken spouse, but she knew she'd blown it."

"Gus, before I forget, I need to tell you that Mary called earlier today."

"She did?" His tone revealed that my statement had caught

him off guard. "What did she want?"

"She was trying to get me on her side . . . trying to make me believe she couldn't have killed her husband. She also said she still cared for me."

"Man, that bitch has guts. What did you tell her?"

"I told her it wasn't a good idea for us to be talking, and I had to get off the phone."

"You handled it well. I'll have to tell Sid about the call."

"That's fine. So what's next?"

"Sid found the son and he's talking to him down at the station now. A judge has granted a warrant to search the Thomas residence for cyanide because of her statement about the poisoning. Sid will lead the search when he's finished with the boy. That's all I know. Oh, I almost forgot. Karen is re-signing the Thomas death certificate this morning. She's decided not to have a press conference. So, I don't know how long it will be before the newspapers get the word."

"Did you have to talk her out of the press conference?" I asked, but I knew the answer. Gus would do all he could to protect me for as long as possible.

"Yes."

"Thanks, Gus."

"You're welcome, Doc. I'll keep you posted."

I VENTURED OUTSIDE to walk Sleuth, looking over my shoulder for the media onslaught, which never came. I wasn't fully recovered, but the fresh air lifted my spirits. This was the first time I had spent any time outside since my drive home from the hospital. My shoulder ached slightly, but otherwise I was healing well, at least physically.

Shirley came by later in the afternoon and dropped off a casserole. She stayed only briefly because she said she had other errands to run, but she gave me a motherly hug and a tearful goodbye before she left. I assured her that I would be just fine and that I hadn't lived this long to give up now. After eating dinner, I tried to watch television for a few hours, but I couldn't stay focused. I realized that I was going to have a lot of time on my hands and if I didn't find something to do, I'd end up driving myself crazy.

Unfortunately, there wasn't much I found intriguing besides my work and Sleuth. At one time I thought I might be interested in learning something about my ancestors, especially the ones who could have been involved with the settling of the West. Maybe I could go to the library and do a little research on that. Either that, or I could buy a computer and do my own research at home. I had a computer at work, but not at home. Maybe I could get out in the next couple of days. The television was starting to get on my nerves.

30

The media hadn't found out about the investigation of Mary and her son, or the search of the Thomas house, but they did find out that Karen had revised Dr. Thomas's death certificate from accident to homicide. Someone must have leaked the news to the press because no statements had been made by the medical examiner's office or law enforcement. When the revision was discovered, all hell broke loose. The Thomas murder was once again big news. The following morning the headlines were predictably dramatic: "Doctor Murdered. Killer at Large." The radio stations led off each hourly newscast with the story.

GUS CAME BY at 7:00 and caught me in my seedy old bathrobe at the kitchen table, reading the front-page article for the third time.

"What are you doing here?" I asked when I opened the door.

"Thought you might need a bagel," he said, holding up the bag as he walked in the door.

I glanced over his shoulder and saw a news van out in the street setting up some camera equipment.

"Don't pay any attention to them," Gus remarked as I closed the door. "They'll camp out there awhile until they get bored. Just stay in the house today, and they'll be gone before dinner."

Prior to this event, the media would never have dared to phone me at home, much less set up their equipment practically in my driveway. I released all news out of the medical examiner's office, and I refused to be interviewed or even questioned at home. I thought I deserved at least that much privacy. At this point I wasn't sure how much they knew, but I certainly wasn't going to be the one to enlighten them. I hoped they hadn't heard anything about Mary and me. I was probably deluding myself, but I hoped I could keep my private life private, at least until there was a trial. And even then, our relationship would only be discovered if Mary was charged with Dr. Thomas's murder.

Gus eventually broached the real reason he came by. He wanted to tell me the latest about Mary and her son.

"The boy and the housekeeper were interviewed yesterday."

"Did they know anything?" I was silently hoping that if one or both were involved, Mary might be eliminated as the major suspect.

"It was obvious that the housekeeper didn't know anything.

We're pretty sure the boy wasn't involved with killing his father. We leaned on him pretty hard. He's lawyered up now so we don't have any more shots at him, but Sid doesn't feel he was involved. His connection to Brower is just what you suspected."

"Was it really the gambling debts?"

"So far as we know. He said both his parents had known about his problem and were giving him hell, but they were also helping him pay off the debts. After his father's death, he unloaded on his mom that his debt was even bigger than he'd originally confessed. But then he said something strange happened, and Brower let him off the hook, saying his account was paid in full. He didn't know what to make of that, but he wasn't about to look a gift horse in the mouth. Later on though, he figured it out."

"What are you talking about?"

"He's convinced that Brower and his mother were having an affair. He said that before his father's death, his parents had been fighting a lot, and his mother had taken to being gone at all hours of the day and night. Dr. Thomas was the kind of man who expected his wife to attend all of the requisite social events for a doctor's wife, and he was annoyed that she wasn't doing her share to keep up appearances. He kept questioning the boy about his mother's activities during the day, which made John Jr. more observant than he might otherwise have been. He overheard several rather romantic conversations between her and someone other than her husband, and once he even happened to see her car in Brower's driveway. He put two and two together and figured it out. The boy finally confronted her, and she didn't deny the relationship."

It was as if a gun had gone off in my brain. I looked at Gus with an aching honesty. "I believed in her, Gus. I believed every word her pretty little mouth sent my way. And now it's all starting to make sense."

While the thought of Brower and Mary making love instantly made me nauseous, I tried to stay focused on the bigger picture. So much of the puzzle was clear to me now. That was Mary's car I'd seen in Brower's driveway. All of her hesitancy to be with me was just a ploy to keep me at arm's length while she continued her affair with Brower. The evening of sex with me was merely staged to convince me to change the death certificate, awarding her with all the money she and her lover could ever want. She'd poisoned her husband to get him out of the way so she and Brower could spend their time together in the kind of luxury she was accustomed to. The scenario was so ugly, it almost seemed laughable.

I recovered enough to ask, "So what's going to happen now?"

"I think that Mrs. Thomas will eventually be charged with her husband's murder. We really don't have good evidence other than the cyanide in the Thomas drug screen. No cyanide was found in the house. All the circumstantial evidence we have about the affair and your part in all this will make a good case."

"When do you think she'll be arrested?"

"I don't know." It was obvious Gus wasn't involved with that part of the investigation.

"I will tell you that the prosecutor will be handling the case herself. She might be giving you a call."

Gus left shortly thereafter. He was accosted in the front

yard by the media, but he skillfully brushed them aside. The media hadn't come any closer to the house than the sidewalk. I was surprised they weren't hammering on the door, bombarding me with questions. Once again, I thought Gus might have had something to do with that.

Later, I received a call from the prosecutor, Stephanie Struttman. She wanted to come by and talk to me about the case. I told her anytime was fine since I wasn't leaving the house. I suggested she might want to come in the evening to avoid the media. Ms. Struttman followed my advice and arrived precisely at 7:15 P.M.

When I answered the bell, I could see that the media trucks and vans had disappeared. I invited the prosecutor in. She was very apologetic.

"I'm sorry I'm so late. But I had quite a bit to do at the office and couldn't get away until just a while ago."

I wasn't surprised that she'd been working late. She had a reputation for being a tireless attorney who would work straight through the night to prepare for a case or a day in court. She was in her second term as county prosecutor. When elected, she was the youngest person and first woman to hold that position in Greene County. She graduated with honors from the Washington University School of Law in St. Louis and had decided after just a few years in private practice that she wanted to be a prosecutor.

I asked her to take a seat on the sofa and offered her coffee, which she politely refused. She said she avoided caffeine because it interfered with her daily workouts. I had heard she was into fitness and upon a closer look, I could see the results. She was a trim five eight or nine and had the muscular leanness that comes from working with weights. Wearing a perfectly tailored business suit, she exuded confidence and intelligence. Her auburn hair was pulled back into a severe ponytail, and I realized I might have found her attractive if she'd possessed any softness. But she didn't.

"Dr. Jamison, I don't want to waste too much of your time. I'd like to go over some of the particulars of the death of Dr. Thomas, your involvement with his wife, and the death of George Brower." She went right to the point.

"Ms. Struttman. All I seem to have right at the moment is an abundance of time." My humor didn't register. She just stared at me unemotionally with her dark blue eyes.

"Go ahead and ask me," I responded in a businesslike tone.

"I have heard most everything I need to know from Detective Freeman. There are just a few points I want to clarify." She didn't wait for a response.

She began going over the major points from my discussion with Sid, finishing with the details of the shooting and the autopsy. Then she asked some questions about my conversations with Mary concerning her husband's death. I nodded when appropriate. I didn't have to say much until she started quizzing me about my personal relationship with Mary.

"Had you had any contact with Mrs. Thomas between the time you lived with her in college until you told her about the death of her husband?"

"No."

"And when did the two of you become intimate?"

I told her about our dinner together and the rest of the evening, leaving out as much detail as possible.

"Did she initiate the sex?"

"Why do you need to know that? I don't remember. It just happened."

"Were you both drunk? Could she have been faking it?"

"Faking what?" I was becoming annoyed.

"Faking being drunk. What other interpretation could there be?"

"I don't think so." I attempted to remain calm, but I was beginning to dislike this woman.

"And how many times did the two of you have sex?"

"That's none of your business, and besides, I thought it was more than just sex." Now I was irritated.

"Dr. Jamison, I don't care if it was the best or the worst sex you've ever had. I'm not interested in whether it was just sex or something more romantic. The point is, the defense is going to be much tougher on you than I'm being right now. You've testified many times, and you should understand this. Let's continue."

She asked a few more questions, then said she was finished.

"Are you going to arrest her?" I asked.

"To be honest, I'm not sure. I'm considering the possibility of taking this to the grand jury and letting them decide."

"Thanks for the information. And I'm sorry I became upset."

"Don't worry, I'm used to it." She made a hasty exit.

THE MEDIA DISAPPEARED, and I felt like a teenager who's been granted a reprieve from being grounded. I got into my car and began driving rather aimlessly, just enjoying my freedom and the outdoors. When Circuit City came into view, I decided to stop. Within a half an hour, I had purchased a laptop, printer, some paper, and lots of ink cartridges. I was eager to get back to my research on people named Jamison in the Old West.

The computer idea gave me a new sense of purpose. I didn't mind reading the directions and trying to figure out how to install all the software and get hooked up to the Internet. Compared to understanding the world of computer technology, performing autopsies seemed like a cakewalk. After some minor complications, I was on the Internet and experiencing a whole new world. My knowledge of the Web had previously been confined to finding articles having to do with forensic pathology. As my natural curiosity began to exert itself, I became fascinated with the amount of information I could find on just about any subject. I was a kid with a brand new toy and played with it far into the night. I fell asleep so soundly that I barely heard the telephone the next morning.

"Mark. This is Stan Garland."

"Hi, Stan. I wondered when I might be hearing from you." I knew Stan would be calling and it would be difficult for him to tell me what he had to say.

"Mark, you probably know why I'm calling. The commissioners believe it would be in your best interest if you resign."

"Resign? I'm surprised you're giving me the option. I expected to be fired." A part of me was grateful that they were being so humane in their treatment of the famed medical examiner who had betrayed them all.

"We thought it best if we gave you the chance to resign. Let's say we're allowing it because of your long tenure with this county. Your work has been the best. We think we owe it to you."

I didn't want to question Stan about the closeness of the vote and which, if any, of the commissioners didn't want to give me this option. I knew it would be pointless and it might even put Stan on the spot. He had supported me for years, and I needed to return the favor.

"Stan, I only have one favor to ask."

"What's that?"

"I'll resign as soon as you and the other commissioners like, but I don't want to do it in person."

"Mark, that's no problem. I do think you'll save yourself considerable stress if you do it as soon as possible. Can you write a letter and have it to us by tomorrow? I know that's short notice. . . ."

"No problem. I just hooked up a new computer, so I can have it to you tonight by e-mail. That is, if I can figure out how to establish an e-mail account. I'll still follow it up with a formal letter."

"That would be fine, Mark. One last thing."

"What's that?"

"We usually give a going-away party to all public officials who have served the county for a number of years, but in your case, I'm afraid some people might object. I hope you understand."

"Stan, I understand completely." The last thing I expected was a retirement party thrown in my honor. I wasn't that much of a hypocrite. In light of the fact that I had thrown away a great career that I was very proud of, the lack of a party seemed immaterial.

By 10 that night, I had set up an e-mail account and sent the notice to Stan of my resignation. I made it effective immediately. I agreed that the county should be protected from any embarrassment about my illegal activities. Now officially among the unemployed, I pondered my options. I had enough savings that I could survive in Springfield for at least a year, but I really didn't want to stay around. Anxious to put the past behind me, I started making plans.

THE PROSECUTOR CALLED the next day.

"Dr. Jamison. This is Stephanie Struttman."

"What can I do for you?"

"I need to talk to you about the Thomas case."

"Go on." What else would she be wanting to talk to me about?

"I've decided to take the case to the grand jury. We have one sitting right now."

Taking the case to the grand jury was probably a smart thing for her to do. She would let the citizens of Greene County decide if Mary should be tried for killing her husband. If they didn't think there was enough evidence, then there wouldn't be an arrest or a trial. By letting them decide, she would be off the hook if she took the case to trial and lost. She could always cover her ass by saying she did what the citizens wanted, but didn't have the evidence. And if she won, she'd look like a star.

"Sounds good to me," I said, as if I had anything to do with the decision.

"You know you will be our star witness. Maybe just you, the toxicologist, and Detective Freeman will have to testify."

"When do you think I'll be needed?"

"I'm working like hell to get this on the docket in about a week."

"That's pretty fast."

"I know, but I think I can do it. I'll need you to be available when it comes up."

"Don't worry, I'll be around. I really don't have anywhere else to go." I tried to be courteous, even though I knew she'd be sending me a subpoena, forcing me to appear.

"I'll let you know as soon as I have a date and time."

31

The fact that I would be testifying to the grand jury in a week caused me to rethink my decision to leave Springfield. Once I testified, I was free to go. Of course, I'd have to return for a trial if there was one, but that would probably be at least a year away. And even then, there might be a plea bargain, and in that case, I wouldn't have to return at all.

I decided that I would place my home on the market and then make my escape as soon as the grand jury was finished with me. My ties to Springfield were limited to friendships like the one I shared with Gus and a few others, so it would be relatively easy to leave. I had no family or loved ones to worry about. I forced myself to see this situation as a new adventure and a positive move. I busied myself with the practical issues like contacting a real estate agent and putting my house up for sale.

DEADLY DECEIT

One important item I did overlook was my license to practice medicine. I needed to find an attorney who would represent me. Though I knew I deserved to be punished for what I'd done, I hoped I wouldn't lose my license forever. A good lawyer might be able to make that painful time as short as possible.

I chose John Crites. He had been a well-respected member of Springfield's legal community since long before I arrived on the scene. I knew he had important connections in Jefferson City, the state capitol. Of similar age, we'd known each other ever since we had first opposed each other on a murder case. When I called, he didn't hesitate to say he'd be glad to help me if he could. We met over coffee and I reiterated the tortuous story of all that had happened to me. He reserved comment except to say he believed the loss of my medical license would not be permanent. I hoped his crystal ball was accurate.

TWO DAYS LATER, I mustered up enough courage to go to the office to clear out my belongings. I had quite an accumulation of mementos from my long tenure. But saying goodbye to the people I'd worked with so long was the hardest part. It was especially difficult saying goodbye to Shirley. Karen maintained her composure because she was now the chief. Everything she'd ever wanted had fallen into her lap. I didn't say goodbye to Gus because we'd be seeing each other again before I left.

I BUSIED MYSELF with a solitary existence for the next few days until the grand jury met. I spent countless hours seated in front of my laptop, searching through hundreds of Web sites concerning forensic pathology, death, and the West. I even entered some chat rooms, solely as an observer and not as a participant.

Stephanie Struttman called and asked me to be at the courthouse at 9 A.M. Monday morning. She had decided to call me, Sid, and Herb, the toxicologist, as witnesses. I began thinking about my testimony. This would be the first time that I'd be testifying in any other capacity than as an expert. I was the main witness in the state's case. The more I thought about it, the less confident I became. I kept hoping a natural disaster would occur to keep Monday from arriving.

MEANWHILE, I FOUND A REALTOR who assured me my house would sell quickly. I wanted to be out and leave town without a backward glance. The Realtor convinced me that if the price were right, I would be successful. He suggested a price a few thousand dollars under the going rate for a home similar to mine. And he was right. My house sold within five days. The new owners wanted the house vacated within a week of closing, and I was glad to oblige.

ON MONDAY MORNING, my stomach was in knots. This was definitely a new experience for me. I put on my only suit and found a suitable tie. A few sips of coffee only increased the churning in my belly. I stopped at my favorite bagel shop after the I left the house in hopes that my old routine would settle me down. Arriving at the courthouse a little before nine, I was told that the jury would be seated a few minutes late.

"Hey, Doc." Gus's familiar voice approached me from behind.

"What are you doing here?"

"Just thought you might need some company. Let's find a place where we can polish off that bagel you're carrying and my nice warm doughnuts."

We found an empty witness room and spent the next 15 minutes eating and making small talk. His presence helped me forget my nervousness.

While we were munching away, Gus told me the latest on the Hatfield case.

"Karen is going to rule the death a homicide. She thinks the parallel marks on the woman's back match up with the width of the brace on the dolly. The other mark, the round one, appears to have been made by the metal end of the bungee cord."

"Oh, I remember. The cord was attached to the dolly. That's good work. We all knew the husband's story didn't ring true."

"There's more, Doc."

"What's that?"

"We've discovered more insurance policies. We're up to over a million dollars. That's a hell of a lot for a newly married couple, huh?"

I smiled inwardly, satisfied that Hatfield would go to prison for murdering his wife and relieved that I hadn't done anything to interfere with the case.

Before I could answer, I was called into a small courtroom devoid of spectators, containing only the jurors, a bailiff, and the prosecutor. Every pair of eyes followed my journey up the aisle. Glancing over at the jury, I saw a mixture of young, old, female, and male. Surprisingly, I recognized a lady whose son had died from drowning a few years back. She gave me a slight smile when our eyes met. I was amazed she had been selected as a juror because the fact that I had autopsied her son was certainly a reason for her to be excused.

The prosecutor put everyone at ease as soon as I was seated. She explained to the jurors that there would be no cross-examination by a defense attorney, and they were welcome to ask questions at any time. Most of the jurors nodded their heads as if to say they knew who I was when the prosecutor introduced me.

"Dr. Jamison, I think you know why you're here."

"Yes, I do."

"The jurors know some of the facts of the case, but I would like you to tell them in your own words about your involvement in the investigation of Dr. Thomas's death."

I began with my arrival at the scene of the accident and finished with my knowledge of what the toxicologist had discovered during Dr. Thomas's second drug screen. There were no interruptions while I spoke; however, there were a few gasps when I described my discovery of Mort's lifeless body. Some of the jurors appeared more upset by the killing of my dog than the murder of Dr. Thomas.

It was only when Ms. Struttman began asking questions about my involvement with Mary that I began to feel uncomfortable. I didn't want to expose my personal feelings for the whole world to see, especially not for the whole world to laugh at. Fortunately, Struttman skirted the issue, and I didn't feel as though I had been stripped naked. It was my habit to look directly at the jurors, and sometimes pick out a particular person to talk to, but this time I couldn't. I was too embarrassed to lift my head and make eye contact, so I just focused on a spot on the floor and gave minimal answers to most of the questions.

I testified for a long time. When the prosecutor had finished, a few jurors asked questions. One older man with a beard asked a question which must have been on the minds of many of his fellow jurors.

"Doctor, have you ever done anything like this before?"

"Like what?" I asked. I'd done so many "things" in the past few months that I hadn't done before, I wasn't quite sure what he was referring to.

"I mean like signing out a death certificate the wrong way? I don't much care about anything else. You're human, like the rest of us, and we've all been guilty of poor judgment."

"No, I've never knowingly falsified a death certificate before. Prior to this incident, I was extremely proud of my ethical behavior as the medical examiner. I'm sure I made mistakes on some of my rulings, but never intentionally."

The man seemed to be satisfied with my answer because his only response was to nod his head in the affirmative. Some of the other jurors shook their heads as well.

When I was excused, I looked at my watch and discovered I'd testified for over two hours. Not surprisingly, Gus was waiting for me in the hall.

"Gus, I thought of something while I was on the stand."

"What's that?"

"You know, it was just a coincidence that Dr. Thomas's car hit the bridge. He could have died at any time while he was driving, in the driveway at home, or even at work. If he hadn't consumed any of his coffee at all, he wouldn't have died that day."

"I think you're right. And if he hadn't hit the bridge, his death would have looked like a natural death. It's unlikely that an autopsy would have even been performed."

"I guess sometimes we just get lucky." I responded. Who was I kidding? I didn't feel lucky at all.

"You're right."

"One more thing, Gus."

"What's that?" he asked.

"Thanks for being here."

"No problem. What are friends for?"

THE JURY DECIDED there was enough evidence to bring Mary to trial. She was subsequently arrested, arraigned for the murder of her husband, and released on $250,000 bail. I wondered where she found that kind of money after pleading such poverty to me. It was probably just another of her lies. She refused to talk to the media, although her high-priced attorney from St. Louis was not so tight-lipped. His statements were the typical "travesty of justice" remarks one would expect. He let the media clearly see his outrage that a woman of Mary's caliber was being tried for such an inhumane act of violence.

I was still having trouble coming to grips with Mary's involvement in her own husband's murder. Somehow it was too hard for me to believe a woman I had loved, and possibly still did, could have committed murder. I found it even harder to believe that greed and some kind of blind lust for Brower could have been her motivation. But then I always had to remember that my own blind love was what led me to break my professional code of ethics and to eventually find myself in the position of shooting at another human being. Something in my moral Missouri upbringing had convinced me that love conquers all and can only lead people to do what is right and just. So much for those ludicrous platitudes. I'd already begun building a fortress bigger than the Great Wall of China around my heart. Despite all my stupidity, I vowed to be smarter in the future.

WITHIN A WEEK, I'd placed most of my furniture in storage, had the house professionally cleaned, and was packed and ready to go.

"Any idea where you're heading?" Gus asked as he helped me stack the last of the boxes into the small trailer I'd purchased.

"I'm not sure. With no relatives here, I really have nothing to hold me in Missouri. The only things I still value are my friendships, and yours is the most important to me. I'll carry that friendship with me wherever I go. I may look up some distant cousins out West. At one time I knew there was a relative or two in Leadville, Colorado. Maybe I'll head in that direction."

With the loading finished, I ushered Sleuth into the front seat. I turned around and grabbed Gus in a huge bear hug, momentarily afraid to let go of my one true friend. He had saved my life, and now there would always be a special bond between us. In hopes of retaining some small measure of dignity, I pushed him away, wanting to make my getaway before my emotions gushed out of control.

"If you ever need me, just call. You know I'll be there," Gus said with conviction. His eyes registered a mute sorrow. If he'd been disappointed in my incredible lack of ethical behavior, he'd kept it to himself. Always supportive and never judgmental, he was the quintessential partner in a world where loyalty was exceedingly hard to find.

"I know that, Gus. You never know, we might work together again someday."

"I'd like that, Doc." His voice was uncharacteristically mellow.

I quickly fired up the engine of my trusty Toyota and backed down the driveway. I could see my old friend in the rearview mirror, waving stoically as I drove away. I felt like one of the gritty protagonists in a Louis L'Amour novel, badly scarred by life's realities, but doggedly determined to enter the ring for another round. Maybe out West, I'd get a second chance.